His Tongue

His Tongue

Lawrence Schimel

Frog, Ltd.
Berkeley, California

Published by Frog, Ltd.

Frog, Ltd. books are distributed by
North Atlantic Books
P.O. Box 12327
Berkeley, California 94712

Cover photograph copyright © 2000 by George Duroy. All rights reserved. Website address: www.belamionline.com

Cover and book design by Paula Morrison

Printed in the United States of America

North Atlantic Books' publications are available through most bookstores. For further information, call 800-337-2665 or visit our website at www.northatlanticbooks.com.

Substantial discounts on bulk quantities are available to corporations, professional associations, and other organizations. For details and discount information, contact our special sales department.

Library of Congress Cataloging-in-Publication Data

Schimel, Lawrence
    His tongue / by Lawrence Schimel.
        p. cm.
      ISBN 1-58394-049-9 (trade paper : alk. paper)
      1. Gay men—Fiction. 2. Erotic stories, American. I. Title.
PS3619.C38 H5 2001
813'.54—dc21

                                                                2001033425

1 2 3 4 5 6 7 8 9 / 05 04 03 02 01

Table of Contents

Past Tense

I was feeling claustrophobic, so I went to the baths. This is not exactly the best mindframe to be in while there—at least for me. I found myself too nervous and distracted to enjoy the sexy (or not-so-sexy) men in towels prowling the halls with me. I'd look at them, they'd look at me, I'd even be half-heartedly interested sometimes, but I couldn't seem to connect with anyone.

I'd run into three ex-lovers that afternoon, one after another. They were men I wasn't particularly keen to see again, or at least didn't want to let back into my life, for a variety of reasons. So I was wondering what was up (cosmically) that they suddenly turned up again, and all at once.

I ran into Sean first, and he was the least awkward of the encounters.

Sean and I had had a brief fling about eight months ago, in the early fall, that ended because I couldn't deal with the fact that he is HIV-positive and I am not. We met at the Chelsea Gym and fooled around in the steam room. He was maybe two inches shorter than I am, with a nice chest and arms. His cock wasn't especially long, but it was thick; it had a nice heft to it, and I enjoyed just holding it in my palm, squeezing its swollen girth. He was a good kisser—something most men aren't even willing to do while fooling around in the steam room. It crosses some intimacy barrier that makes this sort of anonymous sex suddenly less . . . innocent? But I was glad to cross that barrier. To me it made him fun to play with, so we exchanged numbers later, after we were showered, toweled off, and dressed.

He brought me flowers when he showed up for our first "date"—bright orange and yellow tiger lilies. I guess I never learned to appreciate flowers the right way—the whole idea seems a little wasteful since they die so quickly, and the lilies turned out to be messy because they dripped pollen all over my desk before I realized what was happening. But I thought the gesture touching and sweet. Especially since the "date" wasn't even a whole dinner-and-a-movie-before-sex kind of date; we were getting together just to fuck.

I live in a tiny Manhattan studio, so my apartment is kind of set up for such encounters. I don't have enough space for a couch, so guests have to sit on the bed—even if I don't plan on getting into it together. I sat down next to Sean and we started to kiss and stroke and pet each other, and soon we were rolling around naked, pressing our bodies together and still kissing. We took a brief break to catch our breath.

"How does it feel to be in bed with someone who's HIV-positive?" Sean asked me.

The question really floored me. I was grateful for his honesty. I was really glad he'd told me. It was just the way he'd told me—and at this point—that made me feel uncomfortable.

At the same time, I started arguing with myself over what I do in bed. I thought I had sex with the assumption that my partners were HIV-positive, because I couldn't ever know that they weren't—they might not even know. So everything I did was stuff I was comfortable with as being low-risk—oral sex but not if there was lots of precum, and not letting them cum in my mouth; anal sex only with a condom, etc.

Therefore, knowing that the person I was having sex with was HIV-positive shouldn't change what I did in bed, right?

I wasn't so sure. It certainly felt different. I suddenly doubted how much we truly understood about this virus and its transmission. But I bravely tried not to show how utterly fazed I was by his honest confidence. I think partly I was so touched by his telling me—something that had never happened before—that I didn't feel comfortable letting myself freak out and decide not to go through with the encounter.

Sean didn't have any precum that I could notice, so I did take his dick in my mouth for a little while, but mostly I sucked on his balls, and his tits, and otherwise frotted the night away, jerking each other off as we had done during our first encounter together. We didn't have anal play of any sort, and I let myself cum fairly quickly, so he would feel obliged to cum quickly, too. Our next encounter was the same, but then I decided that the difference between not knowing if one's partner was or wasn't positive and conclusively knowing was just too difficult for me and I called things off.

I always regretted that I wasn't as honest with him as he had been with me, but I didn't have the stomach for it. I said things just weren't working out, and when he called a week later, that I had started to see someone else. He let it go after that, and I hadn't seen him since. His landlord doubled his rent when his lease ran out, so he'd moved out to Astoria where the rents were still cheap and switched to a gym there, so I didn't even run into him at the Chelsea any longer. That streak ended today.

I stopped off at a chic little boutique on Hudson Street a little after five. I was selling ad space for a gay travel guide to New York that was being published in London, and I was picking up the finished artwork for their ad. It turned out that Sean's roommate, Pierre, was working behind the counter, and Sean had dropped by on his way home from work to gossip. He'd bleached his hair blond—it looked awful, reinforcing my feeling that it was the right decision to break up with him—and had gotten a starburst tattoo on his shoulder.

We said "Hey" and "Long time no see" but kept it casual. Didn't inquire too much into personal stuff. Mostly I explained things to Pierre, whom I'd never met before but had spoken to on the phone a couple times about the ads. When Sean and I would make a comment to each other we then made one to Pierre, as if we felt we had to fill him in on details, or make a point to include him in our conversation to compensate for our previous intimacy.

What a small world, I thought, as I walked to the next client. We three each had such different relationships with one another, so it was funny that we all connected—by chance—in the same place at the same time and saw how our lives overlapped.

It seemed an isolated, ironic encounter. But the day was still young.

Running into Dennis was the most awkward of the encounters, if only because I always wondered if breaking up with him had been the stupidest thing I've ever done. Dennis sometimes shared this thought. And the erotic tension between us was still fierce. We've talked about it before—we call each other up every six or seven months—and we both pretty much agree that we were perfect for each other, except for the fact that our lives were going in such different directions. And the fact that, living together, we drive each other crazy because we're too alike in all of our worst traits—competitive, territorial, jealous, etc. These conflicts tore us apart every time we got back together, which we proceeded to do for almost two years before we called it quits for good.

I was standing on the subway platform, waiting for the uptown 1/9 train, when I realized that the man waiting two pillars down the platform was Dennis. I approached and he turned and recognized me, too. We kissed hello—the quick peck on the lips that is the standard fag greeting these days—and made small talk, discussing where we were each going, how long the wait between trains always seemed, and so on. I didn't mention that I had just run into another ex of mine, although inwardly I laughed at the odd streak of luck, if that's what it was. Only in New York, I thought, can these sort of coincidences be so commonplace.

I didn't want to mention my encounter with Sean because to compare that brief fling to what Dennis and I shared, despite our many ups and downs, seemed wrong. Also, I think we were both surprised to be seeing each other face to face like this, standing mere inches apart on the platform, without any advance warning as usually happened when we saw each other, when one of us called after a few months and suggested a get-together. Now we were caught unprepared, and it was like stumbling across each other in the middle of some act we found distasteful but were going to politely ignore. This was merely the rude shock of realizing that we have lives apart from each other, so we kept to neutral subjects as we boarded the train together and only chatted on a very surface level. I jumped up and ran off the train when I realized we'd arrived at my stop, putting an abrupt, if understandable, end to our encounter.

Drew I ran into outside the Big Cup coffee shop, smoking a cigarette. One of the things I'd always hated when we were sleeping together regularly was his smoking habit. Drew is a wannabe jazz musician, pretty in a blond sort of way—but not at all my usual type. He gave me his phone number one day when I was in the Big Cup, and we got together a few days later. The first date seemed endlessly dull—we had absolutely nothing in common. We disagreed about almost everything politically, he had no awareness of anything cultural outside of jazz music (which I don't really follow), and after a very short while we discovered we had nothing we could safely talk about that interested us both.

Drew was also so *straight*, in many ways. He hadn't been out of the closet for very long, and the world he moved in—jazz music—is almost exclusively het. One reason he took the job at the Big Cup was to put himself in a gay environment where he could meet other gay guys.

Anyway, despite the fact that our first date was going so badly, we couldn't seem to end on a good note of resolution, so we hung out in Tompkins Square Park after dinner trying to find some sort of common ground or a polite reason to go our separate ways. I guess neither of us had anyplace better to go, or else we kept hoping—despite the obvious—that things would work out after all. Drew smoked what seemed like half a pack of cigarettes, and I kept petulantly switching sides on the bench because the breeze kept blowing the smoke directly at me.

Somehow, probably because I figured that after suffering through such an interminable evening I at least deserved to have my ashes hauled for my effort, we wound up back at his place. And the sex turned out to be lots of fun. He was remarkably uninhibited about his body and about anything we might do. He was four years younger than me, barely twenty-two, but he was solid in a middle-aged sort of way, with a growing beer-gut. He had that ... earnestness that I associate with straight guys' attitudes and attentions toward women, which I found intoxicating. That intentness, focused on you, can be heady.

Gay men are often much more self-centered in their sex, wanting to be the center of attention, everything focused on their cock—or their ass—and their race toward their own orgasm.

Drew had what I thought was the perfectly shaped cock, big enough to flirt with my gag reflex without setting it off. His skin was so smooth and had a sweet taste to it that drove me crazy, whereas some men's cock and balls can be salty or acidic and really turn me off. I loved to lie on my back, head propped on a pillow, and have him straddle my chest and fuck my face. It was my favorite way to cum with Drew. (His was to cum while fucking me, which I let him do if he double-condomed.)

So even though I didn't exactly *like* Drew, we wound up seeing each other pretty regularly, in a low-key sort of way, and I grew to be kind of fond of him. It all just sort of fizzled out when I took a three-week road trip through New England selling ads, and when I came back he had fallen in love with this drummer from a punk rock band.

I'd pretty much stopped going to the Big Cup since then, and I wasn't on my way there today. I was just walking past it when I ran into him standing outside. We chatted for a bit. He told me he was single again. He asked about me. I equivocated, but I didn't have the heart to lie to him, so I admitted cautiously, "I'm not really seeing anyone full-time at the moment." He told me he had a new band and they were playing next Thursday night. I had agreed to let my sister try and fix me up with the new gay man at her office next Thursday; my sister regularly got crushes on gay men at work and tried to live them out vicariously through me. I didn't agree with her taste in men, but it was a free meal, so I'd said yes to the three of us getting together. I told Drew—who I'd never gone to listen to play while we were sleeping together—that maybe I'd swing by, depending on how late dinner with my sister ran. He let the matter drop, and I excused myself that I had to meet a friend (which wasn't true—I was heading to the CVS to buy shaving cream since I'd run out) and continued on my way up Eighth Avenue.

At this point, I was feeling decidedly uncomfortable by the way so many of my ex-lovers were showing up in my life again, in such rapid succession. I began to worry who might be next.

In an effort to stave off any more such encounters and looking for the ease of anonymous sex I went to the West Side Club. I sought the physical release of fucking without any of the emotional foreplay and baggage that come with even a one-night stand, with its possibility of something more.

With all these memories crowding my head, it was no surprise that I wasn't connecting with any of the ready-and-willing guys before me. My libido was hard-wired to the past. I kept comparing the men before me to my exes—all of them, not just the three I ran into today.

A man standing with his arms crossed at one intersection of hallways had Emilio's eyes. Another had Jonathan's pouty lips. And one guy standing in a darkened corner looked exactly like Dennis. He smiled when he saw me looking at him, and I felt an echo of the sexual tension I'd felt earlier today, when I ran into Dennis and found that the link between us—at least physically—was still strong. This, I thought, was what I'd come here for, a chance to relive this memory—even though nothing would live up to the real thing, and certainly not to my memories of it, edited over the years so that all I remembered were the highlights. What could compare with that?

But I smiled back and moved closer, and that's when I realized it wasn't just someone who looked like Dennis, it was Dennis.

"Well, well," he said, reaching out to put a hand on my chest as if we were any two strangers making our first contact. He pinched my left nipple, rolling it between his fingers as he continued to talk. "Twice in one day, after—how long? What can this mean?"

I couldn't remember how long it had been. I could hardly think about what he was saying, almost didn't register that he was asking a question, even rhetorically. His hand felt so good, I didn't want him to stop, but at the same time a part of my brain was shouting that this was a bad idea, that things would be so messy and painful, emotionally, if I let him continue.

But I let him continue. I couldn't help myself, even if I'd wanted to. I was shocked.

First, simply the fact of running into someone I know at the baths always throws me for a loop. I experience a moment of utter embarrassment—a literal "caught with your pants down" feeling—even though whoever it is and I are obviously both here for the same reason. (So, what's the harm, really? But I still can't help wanting to blush scarlet each time it happens.)

But to run into Dennis here, after our curious encounter this afternoon, after months of silence since our last meeting.... And for him to ask the very same question—what can this mean?—that I'd been asking myself was almost uncanny. It was as if he'd orchestrated the entire day's events. Or someone had.

As I stood there with Dennis, naked save for a towel, in a place where men go to have sex—pure and sweaty, strings-free sex—I had to question my lack of belief in a higher order. Sometimes it was so much more comforting to believe that the things that happened to me were coordinated by *some* grand design and not just caprice.

Dennis's hand on my tit was like an anchor pulling my mind out of the past and into the present. His fingers pinched, rubbing the nub between their tips, until my nipples were hard little points and a current was running from Dennis and our sexually-charged past through my nipple and down to my cock.

So even as my mind rebelled at the thought of getting involved with Dennis again, I smiled at him and leaned into his hand a little more. He smiled back and reached out with his other hand to grab my cock through my towel. Dennis sort of purred—Mmmmm—as his hand closed around my dick through the terrycloth. My body had always been responsive to Dennis, and he has always known how to work me. No matter how tired I was or how many times I'd already cum, he always managed to coax a new erection out of me if he wanted to.

"Wanna come back to my room?" he asked, giving my dick a tug.

I hesitated, and I hated myself for that because he could tell I hesitated. My body was suddenly stiff with tension as I deliberated, and I took a deep breath to try and relax. What would it mean to go back with him? I wondered. Can we do this without getting entangled once again? Can we have anonymous sex together like the sex club is meant for, despite our past? How would this change our relationship?

Dennis gave my dick another tug, and I knew that right now my body would follow him anywhere he wanted to lead me.

I don't know what it is—we did the same things I do when I have sex with other guys: we put our dicks in each other's mouths and asses, we kissed, our hands and lips roamed over various and sundry body parts until no skin had been left uncaressed or licked. In short, the usual activities of sex.

But something was different when Dennis and I fucked. Our chemistry. Our energy. Our sexual passion combined with our inability to stand each other for any sustained length of time. Something made our encounters and our connecting so much more intense.

That night in the bathhouse I gave myself over to Dennis without any worrying about what it meant for us to be fucking again. As his tongue explored my mouth while he inserted a third finger up my ass, I did not wonder if he expected me to call him later in the week or if we would see each other again; I just lived the sensations of tongue and hand and body and heart. There was no score-keeping of who had cum how many times and in what positions. I sucked his cock until I was breathless and we rested, lying sweaty in a tangle of arms and legs and cocks pressed between our bodies. If he didn't suck me in turn when our rest became sex again, but instead I resumed sucking him off, for once our competitive natures seemed at peace. As long as our bodies touched, it hardly mattered what we did to and with each other.

The desk clerk called my locker number when I went over my time limit, but I ignored him. For the moment, my world was this tiny closet with a mattress and a pile of condoms and packets of lube—most of which we'd already used. No, my world, for this brief while, was the man who shared it with me.

Later, happily exhausted and spent, we showered together, washing each other's backs, rubbing soapy hands over genitals that were tired and raw but trying to grow erect nonetheless. Passersby came to look at us frolicking under the spray, envious or contemptuous of our intimacy in public. I felt like we were young teenagers in love for the first time, innocently believing it would last forever.

I knew it wouldn't last beyond the doors of the club, and to my surprise I wasn't angry about the situation. I remembered all too well our fights when we lived together, even as I remembered the pleasurable times as well—not just the wild and exuberant sex, but romantic gestures and moments we'd shared.

"Penny for your thoughts," Dennis said as we stood toweling ourselves dry in the locker room.

I smiled at him, knowing I had a dreamy expression on my face that was half-nostalgia and half the pure physical bliss of having fucked and been fucked for the past five hours straight. I leaned forward and kissed him gently on the lips, before continuing to towel my body dry.

"I was just thinking about us," I said.

Dennis got a big smile on his face, understanding, and leaned forward to kiss me. Then he went back to his tiny room to put his clothes on.

Outside on the street, the night was chill and calm and almost over. The city was quiet in a way that we normally didn't see it—like the lull before a storm, or better yet, like the anticipation in a theater just before a performance begins.

Dennis and I held each other for a long moment, hugging and rubbing our faces against each other's necks, really feeling our bodies close together.

Then we kissed, a long slow kiss full of sexual longing and tenderness and lots of tongue. I could feel my dick begin to stir, half resentfully, in my pants.

When the kiss ended, we smiled and said goodnight and each walked off in opposite directions, sharing the same sweet memories.

Practice Pony

I couldn't help thinking about the sign I'd torn down from the post office door:

PUT A BEAST BETWEEN YOUR LEGS!

JOIN THE YALE POLO TEAM.

INTRODUCTORY MEETING
TONIGHT AT 9 P.M.
IN THE DAVENPORT LOUNGE.

The yellow xeroxed sheet with this information was riding in my back pocket, folded into a tiny square, as I crossed campus. I imagined myself astride a horse, the feel of withers pressing up against my asshole, rubbing back and forth.... I was getting so hard I was sure that everyone walking past must notice my erection, and I swung my books loosely in front of my crotch, feeling like I was in high school again. Nostalgia 101.

I'd grown up on horseback, riding competitively in dressage and hunterchases until I hit high school and decided it wasn't masculine enough. Even then, I knew I was gay, but I was afraid people would find out. In high school, it's just not accepted. So I did everything I could to pretend that I wasn't. In college, things were different, but I still wasn't comfortable being completely out. There were these football players who lived on my floor, who I had to share a bathroom with, and I was afraid of what they might do to me if they knew I was gay and thought I'd been watching them in the showers all this time, desiring them.

But the idea of polo was sexy—and very, very masculine. Despite the wording of their sign: Put a beast between your legs. Did they know what that sounded like? Could they mean . . . ? I was afraid to finish the thought, lest I jinx myself. I glanced at my watch, then thrust my hand into my pocket. Just eleven hours until I can find out, I told myself, hopefully, as I squeezed my hard cock in my jeans and walked into my Anthro class.

*   *   *

I'd gone to the meeting for the Yale Equestrian Club during the first few weeks of my Freshman year, but when I walked into a room full of women I just pretended I had stumbled into the wrong meeting and fled. My heart pounded in my chest as I hurried back to Old Campus and my dorm; no way was I going to be the only boy on an all-women team! That would've been like running through the streets shouting, "I'm a faggot! I'm a faggot!" and I wasn't ready for that. I'm still not, although I'm much farther out of the closet than I was last year.

I didn't think the Polo Team would be anything like the Equestrian Team. It didn't seem like a women's thing, so I was surprised to see four or five girls in the Davenport Lounge when I walked in a little before 9 P.M. But there were also a dozen guys sitting about, half of them in riding pants or chaps and boots. There was one man—and he was a young man, not a boy like most of the people in the room—who seemed to dominate the whole room. His skin spoke of some exotic clime: Brazil or Argentina, someplace Latin, someplace where heat and passion are a way of life. He had liquid black eyes and lips that curled in a small pout when he stopped talking. Obviously tall, even though he was sitting on a couch, his long legs were casually spread wide. . . .

I quickly looked away. Great first impression, I berated myself, drooling all over the men.

But as I scanned the room and my eyes fell on him again, talking with a group of three very frosh-looking guys in jeans who stood facing him, I knew that I'd be joining the team if he was on it.

I struck up a conversation with someone I recognized from one of my Poli Sci classes, and after a moment Mr. Drop-Dead Gorgeous stood up and called the room to order. He was even more attractive when standing, I thought, as my eyes traveled up and down his tall frame. The bulge in his crotch seemed even more enormous on his thin waist.

Turns out he wasn't just on the team, he was Captain. Which meant I'd suddenly developed a new hobby.

*   *   *

The smell of wood shavings always brings back the memory of the first time I sucked another man's cock: it was a hot summer afternoon when one of the stablehands took me into one of the back stalls and dropped his pants. I'd been so enthralled by that huge, veined piece of flesh that swelled between his legs. It reeked of his sweat as I knelt down to examine it more closely; the whole barn reeked of strong scents: cedar from the shavings, the stale bite of the horse's urine, steaming mounds of manure baking in the heat. Precum was leaking from the tip, and I reached out to wipe it away; my fingers burned as they brushed against the swollen, throbbing glans, but rather than pulling back I grabbed hold of his cock with my fist. It was easily twice as thick as my own, I marveled, and half again as long. I'd hardly imagined cocks could be that size. "Suck on it," the stablehand commanded, pulling my head toward his crotch. There was no way I could take it, I thought, but as I opened my mouth to protest his cock pushed in and—

I shifted uncomfortably in my jeans, suddenly very aware of my surroundings in the Yale Armory. My cock was stiff as a polo mallet, and feeling far too confined in the jockey shorts I was wearing instead of boxers. I'd want the support, I knew, once I was on horseback; I hadn't made allowances for getting such a raging hard-on. And staring at the Captain's tight ass in his riding chaps as we followed him to the arena wasn't helping it go away!

There were eleven of us left, after listening to the requirements for being on the team and the commitment we'd have to make if we joined. We were now about to try getting up on horseback. Many had never ridden before, so it was a chance for them to see what it was like, to get used to being astride a living creature. There were only four horses saddled up in the arena, so we took turns getting on and walking around. To keep us humble, as if simply staying astride weren't battle enough, we had to walk forward and try to hit a ball. Just holding onto the mallet was tricky. I rode English, but you had to keep the reins bunched in one hand and neck rein like in Western styles, so that your right hand was free to hold the mallet. It looked so easy when the team did it, but when I tried to hit the ball I must've missed by four feet!

I kept guiding my horse around again, in tight circles, again and again, trying to hit that damned ball. But I never did. The mallet struck too high or too low or too far to one side. I was really impressing the Captain like this, I told myself each time, trying hard to fight the blush of shame and embarrassment that colored my cheeks.

To my surprise, as I dismounted the Captain said, "You've got a good seat and you ride well. But you can't hit the ball for shit. Meet me in the practice room at the gym tomorrow at six-thirty."

My heart was beating so hard and loud that I couldn't hear my own reply. I must've mumbled something. He hadn't offered anyone else a private lesson, so he must actually see something in me. My cock felt pinched in my jockeys again. I wanted to climb up into the hayloft and jerk off, but I didn't know how to get up there yet. I went into the bathroom instead. My hand was covered with grime and horsehair but I didn't care; I fisted my stiff cock until I came, whispering "Alberto" as I shot my load against the white ceramic of the sink.

*   *   *

Classes were done for the day, so the gym was crowded not only with sports teams practicing, but also a large number of people who were there simply to work out or jog or swim. I wished I had an excuse to cruise through the locker rooms and get an eyeful of the sweaty jocks going into the showers, but I was fully dressed in my riding gear, even though I wasn't about to be on horseback, just the wooden practice horse. I thought it would make a better impression on the Captain, however, to show him I was seriously interested. Which I was—in him more than the sport!

I wandered down corridors, following the directions the guard downstairs had given me. Past the squash courts … there, on the end. A normal-sized door with a small window at eye level. I peered in. It was empty, save for the large wooden horse in the center of the floor. I tried the handle and the door swung in. The air was stale; the room hadn't been used in a while. Mallets lined one wall, along with a few old balls that had lost their firmness.

I walked over to the horse, a simple wooden frame with stirrups on leather straps dangling from either side. I swung up onto it and just sat there for a moment, enjoying the feel of such a wide body between my legs. I put my hands on the wooden withers and rubbed back and forth, scratching my asshole through the fabric of my jeans and underwear. I imagined Alberto licking my ass, working my hole with his tongue to prepare the way for his cock. . . .

I checked my watch, wondering where he was. I was still fifteen minutes early. In my excitement to see him, I'd made certain I wasn't late!

I ran my hand up the inside of my thigh, rubbing the side of my swollen cock, which had poked free from the confines of my briefs. I wondered how soon he'd show up; did I have time to go jerk off? It would let me concentrate on the lesson at hand. But even if there was time, where could I do it? I looked over my shoulder at the tiny window in the door. Even though not many people came all the way down to the end of the corridor, it would be just my luck that someone would.

I dismounted and walked over to the wall to select a mallet. I would practice my swing to take my mind off my aching cock. If I didn't lose this erection by the time Alberto showed up there'd be no way he couldn't notice it. I chose the longest mallet and climbed back on the wooden horse. I stood up in the stirrups like they'd shown us yesterday and took swing at an imaginary ball. The mallet cracked against the side of the horse and I winced at the sound. I was glad no one else was here, and also that I wasn't on a real horse! I took another swing and this time managed to avoid hitting the horse, although I still couldn't direct the mallet where I wanted it.

Again and again I swung, trying to get accustomed to the heavy weight at the tip of that long stick, its arc as it traveled toward the imaginary ball.

"Your mallet is too long."

I was on the follow-through of a swing and I almost swung myself right over the side of the horse.

I turned around. My heart was beating from fear, and it wanted to stop completely as I stared at him. He was so hot! He was a tall shadow in the dusty light; dark hair, dark skin, and those liquid dark eyes. . . .

So much for having forgotten my erection, I thought, as I twisted back to resume my proper seat and break eye contact. "I didn't realize you were there."

He walked toward me; I could feel his presence behind me, just beside the horse. He exuded an energy, something sensual that sent an electrical charge through my body. My swollen cock thumped against my leg each time he spoke, vibrating to the timbre of his voice.

"I told you six-thirty. That was ten minutes ago."

My eyes flicked to meet his; he'd been watching me for ten minutes! I couldn't read anything from his expression, so I looked away, down at my hands in my lap, the reins bunched between them and the mallet jutting off to one side like a giant erection. I let the tip of the mallet dip; it helped to hide my real erection.

Alberto took hold of the mallet and handed me another

one. "This is a better size for you." The new stick was half a foot shorter. I leaned over the side of the horse and stretched so far toward the floor that I almost slid off.

Alberto laughed, a short quiet burst of sound. "Much better." I turned to look at him, and he met my stare. I couldn't read him at all, which was part of what I found so sexy about him. He was a cipher.

"You've got to stand up in your seat when you swing."

He offered no more explanation, so I went ahead and tried it, assuming that's what he wanted me to do. I stood up and leaned forward to take a swing, and it *was* much easier to keep the head of the mallet focused where I wanted it to go. I wasn't entirely convinced it was the length of the mallet, although the shorter mallet was lighter. However, I'd just spent a good twenty minutes swinging that first mallet, so I felt some of my skill was simply the result of my own practice.

I took another swing with the new mallet, and then another. Alberto didn't say anything, just watched me from beneath those dark, brooding eyes. I kept practicing. Occasionally he would comment, in the form of an instruction. "Slow down the swing." "Lift your arm higher."

"Take off your jeans."

I looked at him, surprised. Had I heard him correctly? My heart was beating so fast I could hear nothing else. At last, this was the moment I'd been hoping for! Why was I hesitating?

I dismounted and looked up at him. He hadn't moved. He was watching me, casually, almost disinterestedly, waiting. But he was watching me.

I stripped down for him, peeling off my chaps slowly, giving him a bit of a show. I undid the buttons of my jeans and remembered suddenly that I'd shaved off all my pubic hair the other week. What would he think? I worried, as I stripped off my underwear with my pants. As I bent over to step out of each leg my erection was pointing straight at him, so hard it was throbbing like a discotheque. I couldn't believe what I was doing; this was a public gym! What if someone walked past and looked in? But right then, I couldn't care about anything but Alberto and what he wanted from me.

Naked from the waist down, I climbed back atop the practice horse and stood up in the stirrups, my ass up in the air as it had been when he asked me to take off my pants. My sphincter twitched, anticipating the feel of him sliding into me. I thought of him using his crop as a dildo, thrusting the long black leather whip into me. . . . A bead of precum dripped onto the saddle.

Pain flashed across my buttcheeks!

I spun around, almost falling to the floor before I realized where I was and caught my balance in the stirrups. I sat down and gripped with my knees to keep my seat. My ass burned against the wooden horse, a strip of heat-pain.

He'd whipped me!

"I didn't tell you to take your chaps off," he said.

I dismounted again. He was standing much nearer to me this time. I could feel the closeness of his body, making my own respond strongly. He saw all of me, naked before him, so obviously desiring him, but he made no move toward me. I had to wonder what he planned to do with me, or to me. Whatever it was, my body wanted it and was ready for him.

I bent down to pick up my chaps and couldn't help looking at his basket, which always bulged so prominently that I couldn't even tell if he was hard now or not. I climbed back into my leathers, pulling them over my legs. My ass and cock were left bare, and it felt as if a sudden draft snuck through the tiny window, deliciously cold and making me even harder.

I climbed back onto the practice horse and resumed my position in the stirrups, leaning forward over the neck, my ass thrust into the air.

He tapped the inside of my leg with the crop and I tried not to flinch. Slowly, he tapped his way up my inner thigh, sending goosebumps across my skin.

He tapped my balls, on either side, making them swing.

He didn't say anything about the stubble.

Suddenly the crop was gone. I wanted to turn around and see what he was doing, but I stayed where I was. I strained to hear what he was doing, listening for a rustle of fabric, a footstep, anything, but there was no sound of any sort—I couldn't even hear if he was in the room with me.

There was a rush of movement behind me, and as I sat down to turn about—I sat right onto his cock. I cried out, unprepared for this impaling. Heat flared through my gut. I hadn't even heard him move, not to unzip his pants, or unroll the condom he was wearing, nothing. His cock was long and thin, like his body; I could feel it inside me, well above my navel, it seemed.

"Grip with your knees."

I did so, pulling myself up off his cock a few inches. I held there a moment, and then he stood up in the stirrups to slide into me once more, pushing me forward with a grunt. I leaned into the wooden neck again, wrapped myself around it and held on for dear life.

He laced his fingers through my hair and jerked my head back, so his hot mouth could more easily find mine and force it open. My jaw ached as his long tongue snaked its way down my throat. He reached under my shirt and seized a nipple between his thumb and forefinger.

I arched my back with the sudden pain. Alberto thrust into

me, grinding forward. My cock slapped painfully against the polished wood. I reached down and grabbed the reins; I looped the leather cords over my balls so every forward thrust made them tug my cock.

His breath was hot in my ear, pulsing rapidly in horse-like bursts from his nostrils. I couldn't hold back; I'd been so excited thinking about him for so long, I shot my load onto the horse's neck, letting it ooze down the wood. He didn't stop thrusting into me, riding my ass relentlessly, thrusting into me deeper and deeper. My insides felt like they were being torn apart. But he didn't stop, and soon my cock grew hard again with his filling me up.

At last, he too came, crying out in a short bark as his body spasmed, then silence. His long cock was still within me, upholding me and holding me up.

He dismounted, and I slid down against the wooden horse. My ass burned; it twitched against the smooth polished wood. I collapsed against the wooden neck, my cock slicked by my own cum as it slid between my stomach and the wood.

"You've got a good seat," he said. "But you've still got to practice your swing."

The Minyan

Simon felt self-conscious as he walked down East 10th Street. He wondered if everyone could tell that he was going to a sex party, which was a ridiculous thought since it was a private party being held at someone's apartment. It wasn't as if he were going to one of those clubs where anyone watching him enter or leave would know what he was up to.

Still, he felt like it was obvious. Which may have simply been because he was nervous. He didn't usually go to sex parties, but one of the guys from Congregation, Uri, had invited him. Simon had spent the rest of the service wondering which of the other guys Uri had invited as well. He found himself mentally undressing the men around him, wondering what they would look like naked, how big their dicks were, if Isaac was hairy all over, thick matts of fur covering his body. He'd imagined them in all sorts of sexual poses and situations.

As if he didn't feel that these thoughts—so improper in *shul*—were sacrilege enough, Simon had been embarrassed by his body's behavior, by the fact that he'd had a hard-on pressing its way outward in his pants every time he stood. He'd felt like he was back in high school, getting a woody on the way to class and holding his schoolbooks in front of his crotch, as if everyone—especially all the other guys—didn't know what that meant. The instinct to shut the *siddur* and hold it protectively in front of his crotch, to shield his erection from view, was still strong, but Simon resisted. He recited the responses from memory, his vision blurring as he nervously glanced to his left and his right, trying to see from the corners of his eyes if anyone had noticed his arousal. He was grateful for the fringe of his *tallis,* which hid his boner behind its white veil, although he was afraid that his hard-on was making the fringe stand out as well.

Although he was not certain who among the congregation was also invited—the way one did not know who exactly the *lomed vuvnick* were—Simon had skipped services two nights ago because he felt too ashamed about seeing those men there and knowing what they planned to do this evening. Or what he imagined they planned to do; Simon wasn't quite sure what it would be like, since he didn't often go to this sort of party. In fact, he'd never been to one like this, although he had once been to a "sauna" when he was down in Puerto Rico on vacation. He'd been fascinated to be in the presence of sex, to watch men around him sucking and fucking in public, but he was too nervous to let anyone touch him, let alone do anything more. Men did touch him sometimes—the rules seemed to be touch first, ask later—but Simon always shied away from the groping hands, and the men who tried to sink to their knees before him. He'd fingered his own dick behind the protective curtain of his towel, too afraid to show it off in public despite the naked bodies all around him, and he came almost immediately, shooting into the terrycloth fabric. He went back to his little cubicle and turned the towel inside out, so that the cum-stained side was not against his skin, all sticky.

But he did not leave.

He had felt a compulsion to stay as long as his time would

permit and to watch as much sex as he could. It had taken days of rationalizations and justifications to talk himself into coming to the sauna, and he'd done it only because he was so far from home—practically in another country, though it was technically a territory of the United States. He'd always been curious about the sex clubs back home in New York, but he was always afraid that if he went to one he'd run into someone he knew. It didn't matter that they would both be there for the same reason; Simon would just die of embarrassment if that were to happen.

So now that he'd convinced himself to finally visit one, he stayed in the bathhouse in Old San Juan for hours, pacing the halls, exploring every room and alcove, always watching, silent, not talking to anyone—whether they spoke English or not. He just wanted to be there.

Hours later, in a backroom that was pitch black, Simon did let them touch him. He didn't know how many men there were—he couldn't see them, couldn't see anything. Somehow, as long as he couldn't see them, it was OK. It was like his friend Eric who talked faster and faster whenever he lied, as if he hoped that somehow God wouldn't hear his falsehood if he spoke so quickly.

It didn't make any sense, Simon knew, but he stopped thinking about it. When a hand had touched him in the darkness, he did not jump back. He let it explore, slowly working its way down his chest to the barrier of his towel, tightly wrapped around his waist. The fingers pulled on the flap tucked away, and Simon grabbed the towel before it fell to the floor, clenching it in his hands—to give him something safe to hold onto as the fingers continued to explore, and touched his cock.

Because he couldn't see anything, Simon was able to imagine whatever and whoever he wanted. He was too afraid to do anything to anyone else, although he did from time to time reach out with one hand to feel the bodies of the men around him, the invisible men whose hands and mouths were touching his body, and there were always too many hands or mouths on him, always more than one man. His fingers would venture forth (the other hand still tightly clutching the towel like his own version of Linus's blue security blanket) and touch flesh, drop down to feel the man's cock, then retreat back to the safety of the towel, wiping off the droplets of precum that clung to his palm.

Simon had wanted to pull back, before he came in someone's mouth—he didn't know whose—thinking, "This is unsafe, you shouldn't do this, you don't know who I am." But it was too late. Before he knew it he had crested over into orgasm, his hips bucking his cock deeper into the stranger's mouth, and the man grabbed his ass, pulling Simon toward him, not letting go until his body had quieted again and his cock had begun to grow soft in the guy's mouth.

Stumbling over the bodies around him in his hurry to get out of there, Simon had practically run to the showers and scrubbed his body pink, then went back to his hotel. That was all nearly two years ago now, and he had never been involved in any sort of group sex before or since. Until tonight.

Because he was nervous and had built up this moment in his mind for so many days now, Simon was sure that everyone could tell that he was on his way to have sex.

He was also horny. He hadn't jerked off for the past two days, even though he normally jerked off at least once a day. But he had this sort of superstition about not jerking off on the night before he was going to have sex, or when there was the possibility of his having sex, such as if he were on a date. Or going to a sex party.

Part of it was simply performance anxiety. By "saving up" he felt more secure that he would get hard quickly, no matter how nervous he was, and also that he would have an impressively thick cum.

He arrived at the building and stood before the door. This was his last chance to turn back.

But Simon wanted to be here tonight. For all his wanting a boyfriend, looking for a mate who'd be his life partner, for all his reticence at the sauna in Puerto Rico, Simon knew that he could easily become addicted to such promiscuous sex. There was a part of him that craved that wild abandon, to have sex with many men in a single night, to not know or care who they were or if he would ever see them again.

He hoped that tonight, among these men he knew and who, moreover, were his people in so many ways—fellow Jews, all with the same sexual desires he felt—that he'd be less nervous, more willing to let himself try things he'd only fantasized about. To be part of the groupings of bodies he had only witnessed last time.

Simon cleared his throat, hoping his voice wouldn't crack when he had to say his name, then pressed the buzzer. After a moment of waiting, he heard the click of the door being electronically unlocked, without anyone asking him who he was.

This made Simon a little more nervous. Just how many men were invited to this party that they let anyone up? Or was he simply the last invitee left to arrive?

As he rode the elevator he wondered if men were already having sex or if they'd waited for him before starting. Staring at the floor numbers going up and up, he shifted his hard-on in his jeans, willing it to go down. He thought it would seem improper to have one before he arrived and disrobed, as if he were so hard up and desperate that he couldn't control himself.

Arrows indicated which wing each set of apartments was in. He pulled the invite from his pocket and checked the number, then put it away again. He stood before the door and rang the buzzer. Simon could hear men's voices inside, chatting. He wondered if soon the neighbors, anyone passing by the doorway, would be able to hear their sounds of sex.

Simon heard the flap on the eyepiece being lifted. He smiled, although he always felt he looked ridiculous through those warped fisheye lenses. He took his hands out of his pockets. Uri opened the door.

It's strange to be greeted at the door by someone you know only casually who's wearing nothing but his BVDs. Especially when you're not used to seeing the person in this state, such as if you went to the same gym and saw each other in the locker room all the time.

Simon couldn't help looking him over, up and down, staring at Uri's body. He was short but solid, with thickly muscled arms and legs. His skin shone like burnished bronze, and he had wiry black hairs in a line down his chest and covering his legs, like sparse grass poking up through desert sand. He'd grown up on a kibbutz in Israel before moving to the U.S. five years ago.

"*Shalom!*" Uri cried, leaning forward to kiss Simon on the lips in the typical gay greeting. "The party's just getting started," he continued, "come on in."

Simon reached out and kissed the mezuzah on his way into the apartment. Uri lived in a nice one-bedroom condo. He had a large abstract painting over the living room couch, under which sat three men, also naked except for their underwear. They all looked sort of nervous, sitting separate from each other even though they were all on the same sofa; nowhere did skin touch skin. Simon nodded to Benji, who he knew, and then looked away, blushing because of how Benji was (un)-dressed and what they were planning. He had to suppress a barely controllable urge to giggle.

There were other men, also in only their underwear, standing with their backs to Simon, looking at the books on Uri's shelves. Two of them had kipahs on, pinned to their dark hair.

Uri led him into the kitchen. "Take your stuff off," he said, pointing to the stacks of neatly folded clothes on the countertop. "What do you want to drink?"

At other apartment parties, everyone took their coats off and left them in the bedroom, then congregated in the living room. But tonight, the bed was going to be put to better use. And so, for that matter, was the living room.

There were six other guys there so far besides Simon and Uri. Simon knew three of them from shul—Howard, Stanley, and Benji—although he'd never seen any of them naked (or nearly naked) before. They hadn't been among the guys he mentally undressed that night Uri gave him the invite, but they didn't look bad without their clothes on, just sort of average: dark-haired, dark-eyed, Slavic Jews who didn't get much sun.

Of the rest of them, there was one guy, Darren, who Simon had met before at a gay Yeshiva dance. He was tan like Uri, but his body seemed hairless. It was only later, when Simon was closer, that he realized Darren had shaved it, even his crotch.

The other two guys, Ezra and Joshua, Uri knew from when he lived uptown and went to the gay congregation there. Joshua was a redhead whose arms looked too thin. Not at all Simon's type, but then he never understood the fascination many men seemed to have for redheads. Ezra, on the other hand, was the kind of boy who might catch his eye on the street, with his dark eyes and goatee and v-shaped torso. It was a surprise to Simon to learn that Ezra was shy and unsure of himself, sort of nerdy, hiding behind his glasses the way Simon felt that he, too, did quite often.

Everyone was in their late twenties or early thirties. And they all seemed nervous or unsure of what they were or should be doing. Everyone except Uri, the mastermind of this little get-together, who walked about with complete comfort, unconcerned about his near-nudity and the sex that was on everyone's mind. He played the host but also seemed completely at ease, chatting with his friends as if this were any ordinary get-together.

Since few people knew each other, no one really knew what to talk about.

"It's funny," Howie said. "My mother is always after me, since all my boyfriends are blond and blue-eyed. If you have to have sex with other men, she asks, couldn't you at least find a nice Jewish boy? And here I am, in a roomful of guys she'd approve of, only not about to do anything she'd approve of!"

It was the wrong thing to say, really, Simon thought. No one wanted to be reminded of what their parents would think of they were about to do, for all that everyone there was eager for it all to begin. But what would happen when they ran into these men again in their regular lives? How could Simon ever go back to shul if he saw Stanley, tonight, with a stranger's fingers up his butt? He would never be able to see these men again without remembering what they looked like naked.

The silence stretched on uncomfortably.

Darren told a joke: "So this kid comes home from school and says, 'Ma, Ma, I got a part in the school play!' And the Mother says, 'That's nice, dear, what part did you get?' So the kid tells her, 'I got the part of the Jewish husband.' The mother stops what she's doing and looks at her son. 'What's the matter,' she says, 'you couldn't get a speaking role?'"

Everyone laughed.

The buzzer rang. All noise stopped suddenly and everyone turned to stare at the door, even though whoever it was had to come all the way upstairs before they got to the door. They were all wondering the same things, Simon knew: would it be someone familiar or a stranger? What if this new guy was ugly? What if he was unbearably cute?

Even though only Uri knew everyone there, it was like they were all tired old regulars at some bar, just waiting for fresh meat to show up. Was that how things would happen: one time someone would come in and catch someone's eye and make their move, breaking the ice for everyone else to start having sex? Who would be the first to do something?

Uri looked through the peephole of the door, then opened it. Simon could see from where he was that there were two people on the other side of the doorframe.

"Aaron," Uri said, "what a pleasant surprise. You should have told me you were bringing someone."

"It was sort of a last-minute thing," Aaron said. "Jorge, meet my friend Uri. Uri, this is Jorge." He smiled at Jorge, then looked back at Uri and winked. "We met at Escuelita last night."

This was one of those moments of sex party etiquette. Or perhaps simply party etiquette. What to do if someone brings someone who hadn't been invited? At a normal party, this sort of behavior is usually more forgivable.

Uri looked over Aaron's friend and evidently decided he made the cut. He invited them both in and led them to the kitchen to unclothe.

The whole nature of the party seemed to change with Jorge there. It was the presence of foreskin in a roomful of circumcised gay men. It was the presence of a non-Jew.

Simon remembered how his uncle Morty used to always joke, "*Shiksas* are for practice," whenever he asked if Simon had a girlfriend yet.

Simon didn't doubt that this *sheggitz* would get as much prac-tice as he wanted tonight, since every guy there seemed to be utterly entranced by Jorge's smooth dark skin as he stood in the doorway of the kitchen—to show off?—and peeled out of his clothes.

Once stripped down to their Calvins and 2(x)ist briefs and holding their cocktails, they came back into the other room. There were ten men now crowded into the small area, sitting or standing around awkwardly.

"Hey, we've got a *minyan* now," Howie said. You could tell he was happy to be the first one to notice.

"Actually, we don't," Ezra said. And technically he was right; Jorge didn't count.

But that was for prayer. For a sex party, ten bodies—regard-less of their religion—was enough critical mass to get things going. Uri circulated, introducing people and drawing them into conversation. Not everyone could fit comfortably in the living room—at least, there weren't enough places to sit. So some of the guys had drifted into the bedroom, where they'd started to get it on while no one—at least, not everyone—was looking.

Of course, the moment one of the living room group noticed, everyone rushed to the doorway of the bedroom to watch.

Somehow this didn't seem to be the right sex party etiquette, but it didn't stop anyone.

Simon watched the back of Joshua's head bobbing up and down before Stanley's crotch, as if Josh were *davening*, and per-haps this was like prayer for Joshua, lost in a trance of cock-sucking.

With all of them crowded there at the door, growing hard

from their voyeurism if they weren't already, it didn't take long for the rest of the guys to start touching one another as well. A hand on thigh or belly, fingers cold with nervousness. A hand cupping an asscheek through the fabric of his underwear. Simon didn't really know who was who but it didn't matter. His heart beat faster, he felt a tight constriction in his chest from nervousness, then he took a deep breath and relaxed into the sensation of his ass in some man's palm. He thought for a moment back to that bathhouse in Puerto Rico, where even though he'd wanted to he wouldn't do anything except in the concealing darkness of the backroom, as if sex were something too shameful to be seen. Among these ten men, these other gay Jews gathered together for the worship of the body, he no longer felt guilty about his desperate yearnings for sex with other men, as he had on the walk over here and on so many occasions previously. He looked around him, at the men who were so like him, now lost in their pleasure, the giving and the receiving of it, and he smiled. He was not alone, and he was glad to be part of something bigger than himself, this *minyan*, which for him is what it was even if one of the men was not Jewish. A *minyan* of desire, men who no longer needed to congregate in clandestine secret to worship, but who could love and pray without shame.

"Amen," he whispered, and pressed himself back against the man who cupped his ass, no longer holding himself apart.

Glossary

Daven: The ritual bending of the knees during prayer that causes the body to sway back and forth.

Lomed Vovkik: The term for the thirty-six people who are so pure of heart that God does not again destroy the world with flood or fire or so forth. Because no one knows who these thirty-six are,

Jews are taught to be kind and offer hospitality to all, in case they are one of the *lomed vovnik.*

Minyan: The minimum number of adult males (ten) necessary to maintain a temple and pray.

Shiksa: A derogatory term for a non-Jewish girl.

Sheggitz: The male form of Shiksa.

Shul: The Hebrew word for temple.

Siddur: A holy prayerbook.

Tallis: A ceremonial scarf.

Season's Greetings

It had been a long time since I could remember snow in November, but it was hardly unheard of for New York City. The weather had been so wonky the past few years, with global warming and El Niño and whatever new phenomenon they were blaming now, that I wasn't really surprised by anything that fell from the sky any more, no matter the season.

I was surprised, however, as I checked my mailbox while waiting for the elevator to discover that I'd received my first Christmas card of the year. I know that traditionally the Christmas sales season starts the day after Thanksgiving and all that, but this was way too early for a card. I briefly contemplated waiting a few weeks before opening it, when Christmas felt like it was in high gear, but I've never been good about delayed gratification. When I was younger, I'd sneak into the living room when no one was looking, pick up my presents under the tree, and shake them to try to determine what was inside, even though I knew I'd be in big trouble if I opened them before Christmas Day itself. I could, however, wait until I got upstairs and warmed up a bit before opening the card; after all, I knew from the postmark that it was from John.

I stomped my waterproof boots on the mat outside my apartment door, then took them off so I didn't track snow inside. I took off my hat and gloves and scarf and jacket and one of the sweaters I was wearing, and put a pot of water on to boil for tea. I looked at the AIDS benefit calendar hanging on the fridge, with black and white photos of naked men by Jeff Palmer, and confirmed that it was indeed the 29th of November—far too early to be getting Christmas cards.

I took the pile of mail and sat down on the cushioned window seat I'd built over the radiator and hence suffused with a delicious warmth. There was a catalog from J Crew, a bill from AT&T, and two different envelopes filled with coupons from local establishments. I opened both of the latter and rifled through the traditional storage and car service adverts, looking for the coupon for my local grocery store and anything new that caught my eye.

Then I opened John's Christmas card. It depicted a foil-embossed wreath and had a preprinted greeting inside that read: WITH ALL WARMEST WISHES FOR JOY THIS HOLIDAY SEASON. John had printed my name and signed his own above and below the store-bought sentiment. That was it.

I didn't quite understand why people bothered to send cards that said so little. Two bucks for the card, 33 cents for the stamp—to say absolutely nothing except maybe "remember I'm alive." Passive-aggressive blah blah blah.

John was a guy I'd tricked with three years ago in Montana on a business trip held in one of those convention centers so far off the beaten path that the rates were dirt cheap, so all sorts of miserly industries liked to hold their trade shows there. John was the stereotypical blond farmboy type, big and beefy and dumb as a post. The sex had been delicious in that purely physical way sex can be, when two bodies are equally aroused by each other and fit together as if by magic. He had one of those cocks that bent kind of funny even when it was hard, and I was sure it would be awkward to find a comfortable position for him to fuck me as a result. But then maybe I know less about the insides of my rectum than I thought, since no matter what we tried (and we tried many variations that night) felt great.

John was tender and sweet and affectionate, even if we had absolutely nothing in common to talk about when we were not fucking. I'd given him my address in New York so he could look me up if he ever came for a visit, more than willing to spend another night of blissed-out pleasure with him if the opportunity arose. I couldn't fathom spending time with him with any regularity. And I hardly wanted to maintain a long-distance affair with him—they're taxing and difficult in the best of circumstances. But I'd be happy to see him again for a fuck.

I tossed John's card onto the pile of junkmail and wondered if he would ever come to New York. He obviously still remembered me enough to send a Christmas greeting, empty though that greeting had been. I thought about his cock and the way it had felt in my mouth as I held it there, waiting for it to get hard for a third time that night....

I unbuttoned my jeans and pulled out my dick, thinking about John and the sex we'd had. It didn't take long for me to have a full erection. I remembered again the funny bend in John's dick as I stroked my own, and I tried for a moment to twist my cock into that same bent shape. It didn't quite work, and I quickly gave up and settled in to my usual masturbation stroke, pulling long and hard along the shaft and stopping sometimes near the glans to rub the sensitive skin on the underside just below the crown.

I glanced out the window at the thick white flakes of snow falling from the sky and noticed that my neighbor across the street was watching me jerk off. And not simply watching—he had his dick out as well and was jerking off in time to my own motions.

It's a bit of a shock to suddenly discover you are having sex with someone else when you didn't realize you weren't alone. And even though we weren't having what would traditionally be called sex, that's what it felt like nonetheless, even from our separate apartments across an alleyway slowly filling with snow.

I wasn't sure what to do, so I didn't do anything. That is, I kept jerking off, and he kept jerking off, and we watched each other. He had a nice body, from what I could see of it through the storm and over the distance. He was completely naked, whereas I was still clothed with just my crotch exposed. I paused in my jerking off to take off my other sweater and unbutton my shirt, leaving it on my shoulders but open.

My neighbor was very different from John's beefy bulk, which I had just been fantasizing about. My neighbor was sleekly muscled, with nice definition on his abs and especially his obliques. He had that olive complexion that could be from any of various Mediterranean or Middle Eastern cultures, with dark hair and dark eyes and a matt of black hair across his chest but not all the way down his stomach.

I tried to think if I would stop to cruise him if we met on the street, or if this were one of those types of encounters like in a bathhouse, when you're horny and you engage in sex with the most attractive of what's available, often having a perfectly enjoyable time even though you might not, ordinarily, have thought to pick up that given man had you run into him on the street with all his clothes on. Sometimes, in a steam room, attributes that are not obvious in the "polite" world of social gestures and clothes prove to be quite enticing when encountered by the hand, the eye distracted by clouds of vapor or dim light.

I couldn't decide. I was a little nonplused by the suddenness of it, by my unawareness of this stranger being sexual with me before I had had a chance to decide if I wanted to be sexual with him, but it was more surprise than any sense of violation or distaste. Of course, that may simply have been because I thought he passed some ill-defined mark of handsomeness, or because I was horny from my fantasies about John and from not having had sex or jerking off in a few days.

I watched the way his arm flexed as he tugged on his dick, which curved gently upward in the classic erection. My own dick was more direct, sticking straight out from my crotch at a perpendicular angle. I shifted so I was kneeling on the window seat and pressed my dick up against the windowpane, so my new friend could see it better. The glass was cold, making me clench my balls involuntarily and flexing the muscle at the base of my dick, thrusting it harder against the glass.

The whistle on the tea kettle went off, but I ignored it. There were five cups of water in it; it would be a while before it boiled itself dry.

A bead of precum oozed out of my dick, white like a little puddle of melting snow. I pumped my ass muscles, rubbing my dick against the glass and making a little trail across the pane as my neighbor's arm moved faster in its motion. I wondered if anyone else was watching, and what they would think, but I didn't really care, caught up in the moment of our sex. I sat back onto my heels, still facing my neighbor across the alley, and took my dick up in my hand again. His hand and cock were a blur as he jerked off with the intent to cum, and I too began to move my arm faster, squeezing with my fingers as my hand slid along the shaft and cupping my balls with my other hand to help with the race to the finish. I felt, for a moment, like a teenager in one of those infamous circle-jerks I had never had the luck to take part in when I was actually that young. Of course, I was born too late to play games like "sticky biscuit" where everyone ejaculated onto a cracker and whoever shot last had to eat the soggy mess. I smiled wryly to myself at the ironic thought that this was almost a metaphor for what safer sex had come to during the epidemic: two men jerking off with each other from across an alleyway. But actually, I felt we had more intimacy, despite the physical separation, than some of the men I'd tricked with here in the Big Apple.

My neighbor leaned forward suddenly, his breath fogging the glass in front of his face so I could no longer see his features clearly. And then suddenly there was a second smaller shadow lower down, a series of white splotches that together made a sort of Rorshach blot image of a dove before they began to drip toward the floor.

He waited for me even after he'd come, a gesture I found touching, especially considering the anonymity and distance inherent in our encounter. He lingered in his window, running one hand through the splotches of his cum as if he were using his semen to make a finger painting for me—or caressing my body from afar, using the window as a substitute for my skin, a metonymy of sorts. I squeezed my balls tight with one hand, clenching that muscle that makes them pull up higher against my body, and pumped my hand faster, wanting to come for my neighbor. And after a short while I did, my hips bucking forward as I ejaculated, although I kept my back arched so that I sprayed lines of semen across my own chest instead of the windowpane or the fabric of the cushions.

He smiled as I came, his whole face lighting up, and once I had caught my breath, I smiled back at him. Then he disappeared from his window—presumably to clean up. I ran my fingers through the viscous clumps of cum that clung to the clipped hairs of my abdomen or slid down toward my crotch, thinking I should do the same. I stood, cupping one hand to catch the runnel of semen so it didn't fall to the floor, using my other to hold my shirt away from my sticky chest as I went into the kitchen. I turned off the stove, then wiped myself off with a paper towel, rearranging my clothes as I finished.

Mug of Red Zinger tea in hand, I started walking back to the living room. Through the doorway, my warm, comfy window seat beckoned, and I thought about my newfound neighbor. "How very interesting," I said aloud before pausing and lifting the mug to my lips. I smiled and, still standing in the doorway between rooms looking out toward the window beyond, took a sip of tea.

*   *   *

I didn't see my neighbor again for days.

At first, I was constantly aware of his possible presence any time I was in the living room, that he might, at that moment, be glancing across from his apartment—or perhaps he was even actively waiting to catch a glimpse of me, as I sometimes did, idly passing in front of the window as if to check the weather and looking out toward his apartment. I thought of him especially whenever I sat in my window seat, as I did often in those cold days that grew shorter and nights that grew longer. But if he sometimes saw me, I didn't ever catch sight of him. Our schedules were off-sync except for that one brief moment of, yes, sex, the intimacy we had shared across the gulf that separates us—both the physical chasm between our buildings and the emotional anonymity that cloaks New York City.

I was intrigued by him, and not simply because he was sexy and relatively convenient. It was so uncommon for someone to acknowledge the voyeurism we all practice. New York being an island, we build upward since we can't expand out to the sides. Buildings are crammed up against each other, and, naturally, we can see into the apartments of our neighbors sometimes, but it is one of the unspoken rules of New York that you never acknowledge this. Otherwise, how could you live in comfort, constantly aware of your neighbors' surveillance? That was my situation, since our encounter—although in this case, I was not perturbed by it and was in fact eager for it to happen again.

The unusual snowfall melted by the beginning of December, and walking home through the streets crowded with Christmas shoppers, I would sometimes pass a handsome man who looked back over his shoulder at me, and we would both stop and turn around on the pretense of window shopping and start talking. I always tried to arrange for us to go back to the other man's apartment for sex, feeling somewhat self-conscious because of my neighbor, certain that even though I didn't ever see him, he must be as obsessed with my private life as I was with the idea of his. I thought my neighbor might be jealous to see me with another man, and then I realized that his jealousy might be a way of my luring him to the window again.

The next man I met who made my dick leap to attention at the thought of what we might do together I invited back to my apartment and undressed in the living room, sucking his dick from the window seat. But I was too distracted to enjoy his body, thinking about my neighbor across the alley who did not appear, and soon I moved us into the bedroom so I could focus on the quite-enjoyable sex with the man at hand and not the idea of possible sex with the one I was obsessed with.

The next time I saw my mysterious neighbor was on December 11th. I didn't get home until late because of the office

Christmas party. I was sitting in the window seat reading the day's mail, as was my habit, when I realized I had a Christmas card from someone whose surname and address I didn't recognize. It was here in the city, and it was addressed to me, but I had no idea who it was from. The card was a winterscape image of ice skaters with SEASON'S GREETINGS printed on the inside. It was signed Grant. I looked at the envelope again for the surname, trying to remember who Grant Hopkinson was, when a photograph I hadn't noticed previously fell out of the envelope and at last I recognized who it was from.

The photograph was a naked shot of a guy I had tricked with a few months ago, in an amateur porno-style pose where he's grabbing his dick low to make it look bigger. I hadn't given him my address, but as we'd had sex at my apartment after meeting in some bar (probably Splash), he must've taken note of the building and apartment numbers and my last name on his way out. We hadn't exchanged phone numbers to see each other again, but he'd written his phone number on the back of his photograph, I guess in case I changed my mind and wanted to have another round of sex with him. The photo wasn't bad, and from what I remembered the sex had been fun enough, but I figured he must be a lunatic, and the whole manner of his trying to reconnect like this, in a Christmas card, without even a real note attached, turned me off to the idea of seeing him again.

I tossed the card aside but kept the photo. I unbuttoned my pants and pulled out my dick, working it until I had an erection. I grabbed my dick low along the shaft and tried to mimic the porno pose of Grant's photo. What is it that makes us so desperate sometimes to be seen as pornographic? I wondered. Is it a genuine desire to be an exhibitionist, or do we rather crave to be desired by as many men as possible and seek to achieve that aim through exhibitionism? I looked out the window and thought about my neighbor I hadn't seen for so long now. What he and I had shared across our alleyway was a private moment between the two of us, even though any of our neighbors could very well have been watching us from their windows—uninvited participants in the spectacle of our intimacy.

He was there again now, watching me as I aped Grant's photo. I smiled at him, waving my dick at him in exaggerated fashion. He waved his back. His pants were already tugged down around his knees, although he still had on a flannel shirt. His dick poked out from between the two flaps of fabric, like the lever of a slot machine. I wanted to tug on that lever again and again like an addicted gambler until I won the prize. But I was too far away to even reach the handle, in much the same way that the jackpot always eluded the gambler—the dream, the aspiration keeps him coming back because he can't have it.

But in a way, I already "had" my mysterious neighbor, possessed him, even though we had never touched, never kissed, never felt our bodies pressed deep inside each other. I pulled long and hard on my cock, watching him, enjoying that we both were jerking off expressly for each other, that we had this curious connection from across the divide that separated us. Only in New York, I thought—although I imagined it was possible that these sorts of encounters did occur in other places. But what was transpiring between us, this relationship, was something that seemed to define the wacky nature of life in New York, a city where these sorts of interactions are more or less commonplace.

I came first this time, spurts of cum splashing against the windowpane and falling onto the cushion. I'd wash it later, I thought briefly, flexing my arm again and again to milk the last drops from my dick, not wanting to stop for anything. I kept my eyes on my neighbor as I came, and he was smiling back at me. I felt I had his undivided attention; he wasn't thinking about what to make for dinner later or whether he had paid the electricity bill yet. He was just watching my body, experiencing the sex we were having in our separate buildings, and enjoying the sensations of his own masturbation playing out what he could only fantasize about from across the split.

When my body stopped trembling, I leaned forward and kissed the window, making a pucker print against the glass. I watched my neighbor, who was still jerking off, but I was in no rush for him to cum quickly. I was half afraid that if he did, I would never see him again—even though he lived so close to me. That, too, was something so New York; there were people who lived on my own floor who I'd never seen in the three years I'd lived here. I studied his body, the way he moved, the way he jerked off. He leaned forward and let his tongue hang down, wagging it as if he were trying to lick his own dick. I wanted to lick it too. He let a glob of spit fall from his lips, catching it right on the head of his dick and then using it to lubricate his fist.

He came quickly with the lubrication, and I filed that little datum for future reference as I continued to watch him. He brought his fingers to his lips, licking the cum from them and sucking on his index finger as if it were a cock. As if it were my cock, his eyes locked with mine. Then he grabbed his dick again and waved it at me, a farewell, before disappearing into the far recesses of the room.

I lingered in the window staring out across the alleyway, enjoying the warmth of the radiator below me and the afterglow of orgasm, thinking about these two encounters with my neighbor and wondering how soon it would be before I received my next Christmas card.

*   *   *

My mailbox remained empty of cards for many days on end, and I began to feel nervous—although the truth is I don't usually get that many cards. I'm a bah-humbug sort of guy and used to think of them only as a nuisance, those obligatory cards from clients and all, but now I was desperate for them. Time was trickling by quickly—soon Christmas Day itself would be upon us—and what if I never saw my window buddy again after Christmas passed? We seemed to have this magical connection only if I had a Christmas card from some past lover or trick. I looked at the row of cards I had placed around the window seat; they formed a sort of advent calendar, marking off the days/encounters we had had together.

I took some comfort in the fact that I had not yet sent my own cards, and I hoped there were others like me who waited until the last minute, whose cards would arrive after Christmas. I also hoped that there might be cards *en route*, delayed by the sudden general increase in mail volume.

What would happen when I stopped getting Christmas cards altogether, though? Would we ever again connect? What would happen if we met on the street? Would there still be the same sexual tension between us in person? Or was there some extra glamour that came from being connected across such a distance, like the emotional safety of jerking off to a picture of your boss in the privacy of your home, fantasizing about him in a way that you couldn't imagine ever realizing when you were in front of him in person, because he seemed so unappealing in the flesh.

On the afternoon of Christmas Eve I came home to find a card in my mailbox at last. It had no return address, so I didn't know who it was from, but that hardly mattered. My dick leapt to attention as I stood in the hallway in front of the mailboxes, contemplating what should transpire when I went upstairs and opened it. My libido was well-trained now to produce this Pavlovian response.

I distractedly waited for the elevator, having to make pleasant small chat with the Irish mother of three who lives two floors below me, who kept going on about how excited she was that her brother had come to visit for Christmas and other inanities. Alone at last in the elevator after the 4th floor, I breathed a sigh of relief and leaned against the fake wood-paneled wall, squeezing my crotch with one hand and adjusting myself within my pants. The card was addressed to me as Mr. Bowes and the postmark was from within the city; I had no clue as to who it could be from.

I dumped everything on the couch as I came in and hurried over to the window seat, tearing open the envelope as I went. The card showed a naked hunk, with a Santa's hat over his crotch. I opened it. It was a blank card, in that there was no pre-printed greeting, just a hand-written note from the sender, which read:

Hi, my name is Robert. I live across the alley from you. I looked your last name up on the buzzer, guessing which apartment was yours. I hope I guessed right! I like what happens when you get a card. If you want to let that happen with me, give me a call sometime.

He'd signed the card with his phone number.

I ran one hand over the hard bulge in my crotch and looked up. In the window across the alley was my neighbor, Robert, watching me and smiling. I smiled back, put his card on the window sill, then got up to look for the phone.

A Blend of Food and Desire

Steve sprung a boner when Erica asked him to pass her the blender. He was at her apartment, helping her prepare a three-course meal for a dinner party with some mutual friends. Which consisted mostly of Steve watching, and occasionally passing her items as she needed, or doing some of the foolproof and thankless tasks like peeling potatoes or chopping onions. Some people have a black thumb when it comes to raising plants; Steve had the equivalent when it comes to cooking. If his boyfriend weren't such a fine cook, he would've starved years ago. Of course, that was one of the reasons he had "married" Robert; Steve's two main passions are for food and sex, both of which Robert excels at.

When Erica asked for that appliance, which Steve hadn't noticed was on the shelf beside him, he just couldn't help himself; he still vividly remembered that night Robert and he first had sex with the blender, and the memory was hardwired into his libido.

Robert had visited his grandmother that afternoon, and she'd given him a Macy's credit slip that she'd been keeping in her purse but had never used. It was about to expire, so he had to use it that afternoon. Robert lost no time in dashing off to The Cellar and came home with the blender. He wanted to try it out immediately, so Steve followed him into the kitchen.

Steve loved watching Robert cook. He found it fascinating watching anyone prepare food—the cooking channel is almost like porn, he often told friends—but in particular he liked watching Robert at work, especially when Robert was making something for him to eat. Something about that intimacy of nurturing mixed with the lust Robert inspired in him always got Steve hard, and that night as Robert set up his new toy was no exception. Robert was so obviously excited by it, which in turn got Steve excited, and his dick leapt to attention. Steve stood behind his lover and rubbed his crotch against Robert's ass while Robert read the instructions.

Steve's cock is one of the few things that can distract Robert from cooking—it has distracted him once too often when the stove was on, and burned dinner as a result. But Robert hadn't even plugged in his new machine, so it was safe.

Robert turned around to face Steve, and they began to kiss. He unbuttoned Steve's shirt and slid down his chest to nuzzle at Steve's right nipple, flicking the silver ring that pierced it. His hands had dropped to fondle Steve's crotch, and he was unzipping Steve's jeans in between squeezes. Robert crouched down before him, pressing his mouth against Steve's cock and breathing wetly through the cotton of his briefs. He pulled the jeans down around Steve's ankles as he mouthed him through the fabric, then tugged down Steve's underwear as well. Steve's cock sprung free, and Robert rubbed his face against it, licking his balls and then slowly working his way along the underside of the shaft.

Steve braced his arms against the countertop as Robert's lips locked around his cock and slid down the shaft. Slowly he ground his hips back and forth, thrusting into Robert's mouth.

Steve was staring at the blender parts scattered across the

countertop as Robert sucked him off, thinking about the whirling blades and how his innards felt as Robert's tongue and lips worked their magic on his cock.

Suddenly, Steve's cock flopped free as Robert stood up. He expected Robert to want some reciprocation for a while, but instead Robert turned around and went back to work on the blender.

Steve was insulted.

He stepped out of his jeans and underwear, leaving them in a heap behind him. The kitchen was Robert's domain, and normally Steve was careful not to mess it up. But he was pissed off. He slid his shirt off and tossed it on top of the dish rack.

"I'm going to go watch a porno and jerk off," Steve said. He sounded petulant, even to his own ears.

"I'm not through with you yet," Robert said, still not turning away from his new toy.

"It sure looks like you are."

"You'll see," he said. "Here." He reached up to the fridge for the fruit bowl and handed Steve a banana.

"This is supposed to be a substitute while you play with your new toy?" Steve asked.

Robert finally turned to him and said, "You're such a bitch today. Just peel the damned thing and trust me."

Steve stroked his own dick, still slick with his saliva, and glared at Robert's back. He was being a bitch, he knew, but he hated being ignored. This was silly, though; he was acting like a jealous lover, when all Robert was doing was trying to set up his new gadget. Steve sighed and peeled the banana. He took a bite, a last rebellious action, and with his mouth still full said, "Here."

"Thank you," Robert said, taking the banana from him. He stuffed it in through the top of the machine, and then plugged the blender in. "Ready?" he asked, closing the lid.

Steve came and stood behind him again, forgiving him, sharing with him his moment of enjoyment. "Sure," he said, "can't you tell I'm ready?" He rubbed his hard cock against Robert's ass as he looked over Robert's shoulder.

Robert flicked the machine on, and the banana was quickly whacked into a puree by the sharp blades.

Big deal, Steve thought. He grabbed Robert's hips and ground his crotch against him. "That was more fun than this?" he asked.

"You have so little imagination," Robert complained. He lifted the top half of the blender from its base and held it before him. "Sometimes I wonder how I could have married you," he said, switching places, so that Steve was pressed up against the counter. "But then I remember."

Robert knelt down before him, still holding the blender. He poured the banana puree all over Steve's dick and abs and thighs.

"Oh," Steve said, letting the vowel shift from one of surprise as the viscous gel touched his skin into one of pleasure as Robert put the blender down on the floor and began licking the banana away. "Mmmm," he purred as Robert licked the inside of one thigh.

"You should taste it down here," Robert said. "Mmmmm indeed."

Steve laughed, and later he did try the same thing on Robert. They went through most of the fruit bowl that night, pureeing items alone and in combinations—kiwi and apple, strawberry and pear—and then eating the drippy pulp from each other's bodies.

And ever since, the sound of a blender—sometimes the mere thought of it—gets him hard.

Steve must've moved strangely as he crossed Erica's kitchen with the blender in his hands, trying to shift his cock within his jeans, which suddenly felt far too tight. Erica noticed and looked down.

"Men!" she exclaimed. "Can't you pay attention? The company'll be coming in fifteen minutes. And there's no time for you to come before they do, so go set the table and calm down."

Steve laughed and said, "It's a long story."

"You'll tell me another time, then. Use the tablecloth that's in the top drawer."

Steve went into the dining room to set the table, trying to ignore the whirring sound of the blender that was keeping his dick rock-hard.

Hansel & Gretel & Gerd

There was nothing left to eat in the fridge, but this was nothing new. At the same time, half-eaten food littered the apartment. Gretel couldn't ever make up her mind to finish anything she started. She'd get distracted by something on television or a new idea, put down what she was eating, and forget about it until it rotted and the smell reminded her. Gerd was always preoccupied with work or his many boys, and he was something of a slob himself, always taking off his clothes and letting them fall in a heap on top of whatever surface was nearby. So it always fell to me to clean up after them both.

The apartment was too small for the three of us, and the landlord was always threatening to kick us out because we never had enough money to pay for it. But we couldn't go anywhere else, because we couldn't afford it. As it was, we were so far behind in paying some of the utilities, they'd been shut off. Like the phone. We had to stand in the street and use the one outside the Apothek around the corner.

Gretel was no use in terms of bringing in any money. Even when she earned some, she spent through it like it was going out of style. But then, what did one expect of an aging black drag queen, originally from New Orleans, who'd been living in Berlin now for at least fifteen years? She and Gerd met years ago at a bar where he was working, and they'd been roommates ever since.

Gerd paid the lion's share of the rent, and as such got the most say in how things ran in the apartment. It also helped that he was bigger, stronger, and louder than all of us. Well, maybe not louder than Gretel when she got drunk, or me when I snored (which I did so loudly that sometimes I woke myself up). But I digress.

I, too, met Gerd in a bar, my first night in Berlin. I was staying at a youth hostel and decided to go to a bar called Anderes Ufer that I heard about from some gay friends in Freiburg. They came to Berlin often for the gay scene, because there was not much of one in Freiburg—which is why I left. I noticed Gerd immediately in the crowded bar and was attracted to him. He looked about ten years older than me, with short blond hair and a rugged face. He was tall and squarely built, with broad shoulders, and even through his clothes you could tell he was all muscle.

Although I'd been noticing him, I was more than a little surprised when he came right over to me and told me his name. I was nervous, because he was exactly what I find sexiest in a man, and here it was my first night in Berlin and I had found someone like him—and he was interested in me! It was almost too much to believe. To make smalltalk, I asked him what he thought of the exhibit by Salomé that lined the walls of the bar. Gerd had no interest in art; he asked me if I wanted to go home with him, and before I could answer, we were kissing. He pulled me closer to him, and I felt tiny pressed up against his body. I forgot about being nervous, or at least my dick did, and it started to get hard as Gerd thrust his tongue down my throat.

When we paused for breath, I said yes.

Gerd nodded and picked up his beer, which was on the table next to us. He kept one hand on my ass the entire time he drank it and then all the way back to his apartment, steering me by subtle pressure of his fingers, as if we were a couple dancing. I was ready to follow him anywhere he wanted to lead me, infatuated with his impressive physical presence. I felt sort of like a baby duck in the way they are said to imprint on the first thing they see as their parent; I felt I had imprinted on this man because he exuded such masculine energy. I loved the feel of his hand covering my ass like that. It felt so possessive, and it kept me hard all the way back to his apartment.

Gerd's cock is as impressively big as the rest of him. When we got upstairs, I looked around the apartment, but it was dark and small and I couldn't see much. Gerd took off all his clothes without saying anything. Once I noticed him, naked, sitting on the bed, I forgot about anything else.

Still dressed, I walked over to the bed and stood in front of Gerd, looking down into his lap. His large cock was beginning to swell, but it was still soft. Gerd was the first man I'd met whose cock was so big that it took some effort to get him hard. But, as I learned that night, it was worth the effort!

I reached out to hold his cock as it slowly grew thicker, lifting it from between his legs. Gerd pressed down on my shoulder, still without saying anything, and I sank to my knees before him. I had a good look at his cock before I put it into my mouth, not because I hadn't seen enough of them in the few years I'd been having sex with other guys, but because I wondered how big he would be when fully hard and if I would be able to take him. The vein that ran across the top of the shaft was nearly as big as my pinkie finger. I could see that the head of his cock flared under its thick foreskin sheath.

His cock was warm resting on my palm. I could smell the

sweat on his balls, a musky scent that made my hard cock throb in my pants. I licked along the top of the shaft until his pale pubic hairs tickled my tongue. His skin tasted nice, and sort of sweet.

Gerd lifted the head of his cock and guided it into my mouth. His cock was bent in a sort of S shape for a moment as my lips closed around him. I pulled backward, my lips still locked around him, and straightened his cock out. I could tell Gerd liked getting sucked off, because his cock began to swell the moment it was inside my mouth, even though I hadn't really done anything. I ran my tongue back and forth along the underside of the shaft, letting spit pool in my mouth. His cock gave a jerk as it stretched itself further. I tasted precum as the foreskin slid back a little from the round glans to expose the slit.

Gerd held the back of my head and pulled me onto him, but gently, his cock sliding deep into my mouth. My tongue was squished by its weight and I wanted to gag, but Gerd's hand held me in place—I had no choice but to choke around his cock, until at last my mouth got used to it. Then Gerd let up on the pressure, and I could pull back. I didn't let his cock fall from between my lips, though; I simply wanted to give my jaw a chance to relax and to catch my breath. I flicked my tongue back and forth, pushing at the foreskin where it started to peel back and expose the glans. Even when Gerd was fully erect, the foreskin didn't peel back all the way, still covering the sensitive crown.

I was starting to produce saliva like crazy now, which helped as I slid back down his shaft—though not so far as Gerd had first held me—moving up and down. I sealed my lips against his shaft and sucked in, trying to create a vacuum, and then continued bobbing up and down. It was work, but I felt good doing it, and proud that I even could. Gerd sort of growled with pleasure, not exactly words, although sometimes a sound would become one, a mix of encouragement and exclamation: "Jaaaaaaaaa."

With one hand, I tugged at the shaft of his cock, until his foreskin slid all the way back. Gerd jerked as my tongue spun across the exposed glans and worked its way under the crown. With my other hand, I grabbed my own cock through the fabric of my jeans and squeezed. But it was too complicated to try and split my focus like that, and I choked on Gerd's cock. Besides, I was too close to coming. I ignored my own dick and worked Gerd's cock with both hands as my mouth slid up and down.

But the action had alerted Gerd, who pulled me off of him and lifted me until I was standing. He unzipped me and tugged down my pants and my underwear, until they bunched around my knees. He turned me around and leaned me forward. My asshole clenched nervously as warm breath touched it, but I forced myself to relax. Gerd's tongue licked my crack, and then he bit lightly on my right asscheek, making me jump. When I relaxed again, leaning back a little more, his warm wet tongue wormed its way into my asshole.

Soon a finger joined it, pushing and prodding at my asshole, which was slick with his spit. He kept working me open, adding another thick finger every time I got used to the sensation, and using enough spit to keep everything slippery. Soon he had four fingers up inside me, pushing deeper and deeper and gently picking up speed in their thrusting. I was moaning like a tomcat in heat and I didn't care who heard me or what his neighbors thought, I just didn't want him to stop.

But eventually he did, sliding his fingers from my ass. I stayed bent over as I was, taking a deep breath to recover from the heady sensation of his finger-fucking, even as I wanted to beg him to continue. Of course, he wasn't done with me yet.

He spun me around until I was facing the bed, and gently pushed me forward. He reached over and grabbed the pillows, piling them under my stomach to cushion me while he fucked me, as well as to keep my ass in the position he wanted it.

There was a bottle of some sort of lotion or oil next to the bed, and Gerd squirted some onto his hands or his dick, I didn't know which, since I was facing the other way. I could hear his hand spreading the liquid along his cock; it made a little squelch from the pressure of his fingers. I heard the bottle squirt again, and then I felt his warm fingers on my ass, with a cold spot where the lube was. He rubbed it against my ass, which was still wet from his spit; three of his thick fingers slid into me with no problem, especially now that they were slicked with whatever he was using for lube.

Gerd pulled his fingers out of my ass and climbed up onto the bed. And then the fat head of his cock was pressing up against me, poised and waiting. I took a deep breath in antic-ipation of his fucking me, and as I let it go he slid inside, just a little bit at first. He seemed even bigger than I remembered, and I was sure I couldn't take him, even though I knew I had been able to wrap my lips around his cock, even though I knew he had almost his whole hand up my ass just moments ago. My ass clenched down around the tip of his dick, and when it relaxed he slid in even further, pushing past the inner sphinc-ter. He was deep inside me and just waited there until I got used to him, before he began sliding in and out and soon was really pumping into me.

I liked that he had worked my ass for a while, making sure I was ready for him, instead of just thrusting into me no matter how I liked it. He was big and gruff, but he wasn't a brute. I felt myself growing even more infatuated with him, and the idea of him, each time his big cock thrust into my ass, pushing me forward and rubbing my own cock against the nap of the pillows.

We were both grunting with pleasure when suddenly I started to cum while Gerd was fucking me. I just couldn't hold back any longer. "I'm coming," I screamed, as my body quivered with pleasure. Gerd didn't stop fucking me, as I squirted all over the pillows. The cum got rubbed across my belly as Gerd's cock pushed me forward each time he thrust. My dick stayed hard, and when Gerd finally came, after flipping me onto my back and kissing me while he fucked me, I grabbed my dick and jerked off while his cock was still inside me, until I shot a second load.

We fucked twice more that night before Gerd was finally sated. I was shooting blanks by the end.

I spent the night. At the time, I didn't know this was such a rare thing for Gerd. In fact, so far as I know, only two of us have ever lasted all night, and both of us are still living with him. Neither of us has sex with him, though, only every once in a blue moon, but I guess the hope of it is what keeps us around—that and the place to crash, although it feels like home to all of us by now.

Anyway, Gretel was quite a shock to meet in the morning. I woke up before Gerd and lay in the bed, feeling how sore my ass was and smiling. I stared at the ceiling because Gerd had thrown one arm across my chest and I didn't want to wake him by moving. I didn't know that Gerd is a very sound sleeper and I could've rolled him onto the floor without him noticing.

The door to the apartment opened, and I would've screamed but I was scared speechless. At first I thought the apartment was being robbed. Gerd and I were lying naked atop the bed. I bolted upright—no longer caring if I woke Gerd—and covered my crotch with my hands. Gerd's arm fell to the bed, and he pulled it under him but didn't wake up. I didn't know what to do, as I stared at this black stranger who had keys to the apartment.

Gretel ignored me and went about her business as if she owned the place. This is something she does wherever she is. She dropped the keys onto a table by the door and took off her wig, placing it atop a bust of Lenin that was evidently there for that purpose. She threw herself down on the couch, where she took off her red three-inch pumps. I couldn't help noticing how wide her feet were. She rubbed the bottoms of her feet, cracking each toe, then stretched out across the couch. At last, she looked over and saw me watching, although I had a feeling she knew exactly where I was the entire time, by the way she had so studiously ignored me until now. "Good night," she said, although it was probably 6:30 in the morning by then, and put one of the couch cushions over her face to block the light.

It was hours later, when Gerd woke up—a little surprised to find me still there—that I learned Gretel was his roommate. The apartment wasn't big enough for one person to live in decently, let alone two. But as I'd managed to spend the night and had no intention of losing such a hunk as Gerd, I collected my stuff from the hostel where I'd checked in the day before and moved in too, figuring the bed was big enough for Gerd and I to share. How naive I was in those days!

Gerd was always picking up boys and bringing them home and making us leave the apartment so they could have sex. Not because Gerd minded having sex in front of us, but because his tricks usually did. Five nights out of seven, Gretel and I were unceremoniously tossed out onto the street for at least an hour and usually longer.

I remember the first week I moved in, the first time Gerd kicked us both out.

I was devastated with jealousy, but the truth is that Gerd simply lost interest quickly, which I soon saw played out quite often. In fact, after living there a few months, I began to grow pleased by the fact that I had lasted as long as I did—four nights— before Gerd went in search of someone else.

"At least you still have someplace to live," Gretel tried to reassure me, "and that's worth more than sex in this town— trust me, hon."

That night, Gretel was wearing a fraying green-sequined flapper's dress that looked like it was a genuine relic from the '30s—and one that wasn't about to live much longer, as sequins went flying off with every swish of Gretel's hips. Which meant a lot of sequins littered the sidewalk as Gretel and I walked down the street—or rather, as I walked and she sashayed— toward some bar she knew of, where she was sure I'd meet a man of my own and find myself a good time.

Gretel was taking me under wing like a mother hen comforting her chick, and even then I had a feeling that this was partly because she knew I still had money, having only just arrived from Freiburg. I didn't have a job, but I hadn't yet run through the money I got when my grandmother died, that had let me move to the big city.

We got to the bar, the name of which I don't remember, if I ever knew it. It was dark and full of men, that much I remember. But I wasn't interested in any of them. My heart was broken. I had found the man of my dreams and he had cast me aside.

I bought us both drinks. Then some more drinks. I got so drunk, I must've passed out, because I remember coming to and not knowing where I was. Gretel was nowhere to be seen, not that I remembered that I'd gone out with her. But eventually she found me, when she wanted another drink. She was already wasted, and I was beginning to feel sick.

"I've had enough, let's go home," I said. I'd forgotten that Gerd kicked us out because he was having sex with someone else. All I knew was that I needed to lie down. And after only a few days, our tiny one-room apartment felt comfortable and safe.

However, I didn't remember the way home. In fact, I didn't know where I was. I needed Gretel to take me, but she didn't want to go yet, she wanted another drink. I dragged her out of the bar and ordered her to take me home. I didn't know then that it's almost impossible to make a drag queen—and especially an angry, drunk drag queen—do something when she's got her mind set against it. Gretel refused to tell me where we were or where we lived.

I got so angry I almost hit her. Instead I grabbed her by both arms and shook her violently, repeating over and over, "Take me home NOW." I shook her so hard that sequins went flying off her dress.

That's when I saw a green sequin glinting on the opposite side of the street, and I remembered Gretel sashaying her way down the street as we came here. Holding Gretel tightly by one arm, I tugged her along behind me as I followed the trail of sequins home.

Gretel sulked all the next day. She refused to talk to me at all, until Gerd kicked us both out again that night. I expected her to take care of me again, since I didn't know my way around, but she started walking away immediately when we got downstairs.

"Wait for me!" I called after her, but she paid me no attention. I had to run to catch up to her.

"What do you want?" Gretel said, not pausing as she walked

briskly down one street and then another. I had no idea where she was headed, although she seemed to have some destination in mind—or maybe she merely wanted to get away from me.

"Where are you going?" I asked, still hurrying to keep up with her. "Can I come with you? Are you hungry? Why don't I buy us dinner?"

Gretel forgave me instantly and I learned my first important lesson in dealing with her.

Having lived with them for half a year now, I know my way around Berlin—especially all its seedier aspects, thanks to Gretel. Sometimes Gretel and I go our own ways when Gerd kicks us out. Sometimes we're not even home when he brings his trick back to the apartment. When Gerd kicked us out one night, Gretel and I decided to go together to Tom's Bar for two-for-one Mondays.

It was the usual jam of familiar faces upstairs, and we said hello to the people we knew as we squeezed our way to the bar and got drinks. Gretel drank hers faster than I did mine, but I went and bought another screwdriver and a free second drink—both for Gretel. I was feeling generous because I'd pocketed a twenty-mark note from the bakery where I work during the day without ringing up the sale on the register.

I left Gretel upstairs with a drink in either hand and made my way down to the lower level. It was less crowded here, although there were plenty of men, most of them standing in the dark shadows with their backs against the wall. As I drew nearer, sometimes a shadow would reveal itself to be two bodies pressed together instead of one.

I walked among the halls and little rooms until I'd reached the farthest corner. It was hot as an oven in that tiny backroom, and sweat was trickling down my sides. I stripped off my shirt, and my nipples began to stiffen as the thick air touched them.

I twisted first one and then the other, sending jolts down to my cock, as I looked around me. It was wall-to-wall men, and in what little light there was down there, some of them looked quite sexy.

I walked along the row of wallflowers, letting my hand drift along beside me, touching here and there. Sometimes I felt a bare chest, sometimes a jeans-covered thigh, sometimes a cock, which I held in my hand, lingering a moment, before moving on. I stopped before one toothsome morsel, because someone was crouched in front of him, sucking his cock. The man being sucked off looked at me—not defiant or challenging, just looking, as if we were both on the U-bahn platform waiting for the train. You could hardly tell that he was having sex. The shadow crouched before him bobbed backward and forward.

I crouched, too. In what little light there was, I could barely see the pale flesh of the man's cock disappearing in the other guy's mouth. I reached out and fingered the man's balls, wondering what he thought of two men working him over at once.

I never got to find out, though, because the guy who'd been sucking him off wiped his mouth with the back of his hand and stood up.

My hand closed about the man's cock, all slick with the other guy's saliva. I tugged on his dick a few times, getting a feel for it. His cock was enough for a handful, and curved upward slightly. It was solid, which I liked. He was circumcised, and I wondered if he was an American tourist, or maybe a Jew.

I took him in my mouth, tasting a mix of the one man's skin and the other guy's saliva. I thought for a moment that this was almost like kissing the stranger who'd been sucking this man off before I did. The guy's cock felt good in my mouth; if I were the other man, I wouldn't have given up on it so quickly, I thought, as I began to push my mouth forward and back over it. I probably would've shared, if it had been me who was sucking this guy first and someone else wanted to join in, but I wouldn't have given up so easily, I thought—even though there were plenty of other men available.

But after a while I realized that the man I was sucking was not involved, despite the fact that he had his cock in my mouth. Or rather, I had his cock in my mouth. He was hard, so some sensation must've been getting through even if it was just physical stimulation, but there was no connection. It was like he was part of the wall. I felt almost like I was chewing on molding, for all the involvement the guy was giving me.

I like a little more action during sex, a little more encouragement that he likes what I'm doing. I can get off on giving a guy a blowjob if I know he's really enjoying it. I didn't know if this was working for him, but it wasn't doing much for me.

Like the man before me, I too wiped my mouth with the back of my hand and stood up. The man in front of me didn't say anything. He just looked at me. It was as if he were mute. I wondered if maybe he was a foreigner who didn't speak German, and thus was too afraid to say anything.

Whatever, I started to walk away. Someone tapped me on the shoulder. I turned around, and there was a tall man, holding his dick in his hand. "Suck my dick," he said, giving it a shake for emphasis.

I was tired of sucking dick, however, and this guy didn't really turn me on. In the dim light I could see that his dick was short and thick and jutted out from his crotch in a straight line. But I was still horny, in a vague sort of way.

"Show me how," I said, putting my hand on his shoulder and pushing him to his knees. He offered little resistance, so I figured he liked being flipped. I grabbed his head and pressed his face against my crotch; he mouthed my hard dick through my jeans, biting down to squeeze my cock. I let go of his head and unzipped my pants, pulling them down below my balls. I wasn't wearing underwear.

He didn't need any further instructions to start sucking on my balls the moment I let go of them. He worshiped one side, then the other, then sucked them both into his mouth with a slurp before letting them both dangle again and working on my cock. He was good at this, but it's hard for me to cum with someone I don't find sexy, and I was a little bored; I wanted to cum and go home. I tried not to think of whose mouth it was working me, and instead squinted at the eye-candy around me. I leaned over and grabbed the dick of the man standing to my left, just to give me something to hold onto while the guy on his knees in front of me worked my cock. I tugged on my neighbor, who shifted away from the wall to give me a better grip on his dick.

And once there were three of us having sex together, it was like the walls came alive, and suddenly we were surrounded by men. I felt like I was in a cage of bodies, and I was ravenously hungry. I wanted their cocks in my mouth and up my ass and filling me up every way imaginable. I wanted to gorge myself on their sweet flesh until I was bloated with sex. I held a cock in each hand, although I no longer knew whose they were and didn't care. Other cocks were thrusting at my body from behind and the sides, so many bodies all pressing closer and closer, and the heat from them was intense. My dick was swelling with the anticipation of release.

"I'm gonna cum," I announced, to give him a chance to pull off me if he wanted to. He didn't let go of my dick, so I grabbed his head and started pumping back and forth in his mouth. I had warned him; if he wanted to take the risk, who was I to gainsay him, especially when it would feel so much better to cum in his mouth? He was breathing faster now, too, and his hot breath tickled my balls each time I thrust into his warm, wet mouth. It took only a few thrusts before I came, letting out a deep sigh as my cock released its first squirt of sperm. My fingers clenched around the cocks they held, pulling tightly each time my cock spasmed and my whole body jerked.

When I'd finished coming, I let go of the cocks I'd been holding and pulled my dick out of the guy's mouth, pulling up my pants. I went upstairs and bought a beer and an extra drink for Gretel, who was sitting under one of the television screens that showed scenes from porno films. My pockets were empty now, but I was getting a buzz from the beer and had busted a nut, so I felt good. When we finished our drinks, we left.

The stars were shining brightly, and Gretel and I followed the path home, walking arm in arm.

Frighten the Unicorns

"I don't care what anyone does, so long as they don't do it in the street and frighten the horses."—Mrs. Patrick Campbell

"Doesn't it make you horny," Phil whispered in my ear as he pressed up against me from behind, "to think of all those monks living here, visiting their neighbors' cells in the wee hours of the night to teach each other the true meaning of devotion?"

My body responded instantly to his touch. It always takes me a while to get used to someone, to the way their body works and fits against mine, before I really respond to them sexually. In part, I think it's because my body forgets what it's supposed to do during the times I don't have sex, and has to relearn everything all over again, each relationship. A body in motion stays in motion, and all that. And in between relationships—when my body is at rest, as it were—it learns to stay at rest. Sure, I jerk off all the time when I'm not dating, but that's not the same thing; I can always respond to my own fantasies, or to watching someone else having sex, on video or in a magazine, and especially in real life.

Phil and I have been living together for almost two years now, and my body is so highly attuned to him that I sometimes get a hard-on from casual contact with him—if he so much as brushed against me while I was doing the dishes, for instance. Feeling his hard cock pressing up against my ass, even through two layers of denim, my dick suddenly leaps to attention.

But this was no place to be having sex. "We're in public, dear," I said, pulling away from him. "And anyway, this was a cloisters, as in a nunnery, not an abbey for monks."

We were at the Cloisters Museum, having decided to escape the bustle of Manhattan without going through the hassle of actually leaving the island. There are dozens of little places like this throughout the city, pockets of calm and serenity that we almost never find the time for. But, on a spur-of-the-moment decision, I'd taken the afternoon off from work and picked Phil up and dragged him here on the subway, for a bit of culture and relaxation. Take the A train.

"Well, imagine it anyway," Phil continued. "Roomfuls of men, divorced from any contact with women for the pursuit of a higher thought, nothing to distract them from the buildup of semen in their balls, aching for release."

He'd moved up against me again, and his hand had crept around my waist, snaking its way into my front pocket, where he was squeezing the shaft of my cock as he spoke. It felt good, but I was afraid someone would notice us. "We're in a public courtyard," I repeated. I had nothing against public displays of affection, but I was concerned about pushing the bounds of propriety.

"They're not paying any attention to us," he said, adjusting his grip within my pocket to tickle my balls. He seemed to be correct; the courtyard was virtually empty, and the few people who were there seemed too preoccupied to notice us as they hurried inside to the dimly lit, air-conditioned room that held the tapestries. I stopped worrying for a moment and ground my hips backward to rub against his crotch. "And there are no horses for us to frighten," he continued. "Now, a unicorn is a different matter."

I laughed and Phil's voice deepened as he dropped back into the fantasy. "Think of all those poor little masochists, flagellating themselves for not being pure enough, as their minds kept dwelling on sin and their bodies followed after. Think of all of them, just desperate for a little discipline." He squeezed my nuts for emphasis, and I gasped for breath. My cock began to throb almost painfully with all the blood that was filling it now.

Phil was getting me all worked up on purpose, I knew, with the story and his groping. He loved having sex in unusual places, and the perversity of the situation must've really appealed to him, this blasphemous idea of practicing a bit of sodomy within the walls of a "sacred" and supposedly chaste place. And right then I wanted nothing more than to let him rip my clothes off and have sex right there, in full view of everyone. But the puritan in me made me drag him off into one of the more remote courtyards and into the bushes. I'm very much a voyeur, and intellectually I think that there's an economy of give and take, but in practice I'm just not much of an exhibitionist.

As soon as I got Phil into a secluded corner, however, I was down on my knees in front of him in an instant, unbuttoning his 501s. "That's it, my son," he said, playing the holy Father as his cock sprang free from his jeans and lifted its head toward heaven. "Let the spirit of the Lord fill you." I licked the shaft, working my way from his fuzzy nuts up to the tip and back down again, loving that strong taste and smell of sweat from his balls. I pulled it down so I could lick the vein that snaked its way across the top, growing thick just before it disappeared below the crown. I wrapped my fingers around the base of his cock and flicked my tongue across the sensitive rim of the crown, back and forth, teasing him until neither he nor I could stand it any longer.

At last, I took his cock between my lips.

"Mmm, yeah," he grunted as he sank into the wet of my mouth. "Can't you imagine it," Phil went on, "THE UNICORN TAPESTRIES from Catalina video, featuring Lex Baldwin repeating ad infinitum, 'Yeah, suck that horn, suck that big horn.'"

I wanted to laugh but couldn't with his cock so far down my throat, so I just sucked harder as he chuckled and pumped his hips so his cock slid in and out of my mouth.

Phil had always been very vocal during sex, and was always cracking jokes about what we were doing. It had taken some getting used to when we first started dating, since I wasn't used to men saying anything beyond the typical porn-movie grunts and lines. I'd thought that was all there was to sex, actually, but now I really got into Phil's verbal play. After all, sex is supposed to be fun.

"If we were really going to enact the tapestries, though," Phil said, breaking off a branch from one of the nearby trees, "you'll need this." I thought he meant to whip me with it, but instead he pulled me off his cock until my lips were wrapped only about the crown—I was unwilling to fully release him— and wrapped the prickly branch about my neck like a collar. "Much better," he said, "your crown of thorns. Who told you to stop sucking, boy?"

I didn't need any further prodding and eagerly slid back down his cock, ignoring the way the branch dug against my skin as his cock swelled my throat. There are times when I'm sucking cock when I'll go almost into a trance, and I've been surprised a few times by getting off from it without even touching myself. One thing I love about Phil's cock is the way it is so perfect for my mouth. Which is not to say I can take all of him in—he's too long for that—but that's one of the reasons his cock is so perfect: it's a challenge, it leaves me always wanting more of it, trying to fit more of it down my throat. And I never get tired of trying.

Phil pulled his cock from my mouth and turned to face the wall he'd been leaning against, dropping his pants as he changed position. I stayed on my knees, about to protest, until I realized what he was doing and eagerly buried my face in the crack of his ass once he'd exposed those muscled mounds to me. My tongue worked its way towards his asshole, licking until it found that tight bud, and I pulled his checks apart with my hands to reach more of it. His sphincter loosened under my tongue's constant probing and massaging, and I thrust my tongue into him, as deeply as I could. I pulled him toward me by his hips, until my nose was squashed flat against the flesh of his ass cheeks as I ate him out.

I could feel his asshole clench, involuntarily, around my tongue as he began to shoot thick ropes of jism against the cloister wall. I kept working my tongue into his ass as he pumped his cock dry, trying to keep my tongue inside him as his hips bucked each time he dropped a load. I couldn't get enough of him, and even after his body had stopped shuddering I licked at his asscheeks, nibbling at the smooth flesh and the downy hairs that coated them.

Without bothering to pull up his pants he fell to his knees beside me. "That was divine," he said, holding my face in his hands, before bringing my lips to his and kissing me. His tongue was warm and wet as it entered my mouth, and I wondered if he could taste himself on my tongue, the taste of his own ass. He flicked his tongue along the backs of my teeth as his hands slid down my body to pinch and twist my nipples, one and then the other, through the fabric of my shirt.

But he knew my cock was aching for him, so he didn't wait long before letting one hand drop to my crotch while the other continued to tease my nipples. He unzipped my jeans, not bothering to undo the belt. By this time my Calvins were so damp with precum and longing, like they'd been dropped in the Hudson and put on without being wrung dry. He tugged them down and pulled my cock free at last, swollen with my desire for him. While Phil's cock stands at attention when he is erect, curving up toward his belly, mine is more direct, pointing straight out from my crotch. Not nearly as long as Phil's, it is thicker and has a solid heft to it. He held it lovingly in one palm and hacked a glob of spittle onto the head. With his thumb, he rubbed the saliva over the tip of my cock, pulling back the foreskin with his other hand to wipe away the precum that had pooled there. He spat again on my cock, rubbing his hand down the shaft to spread the saliva out, then without preamble took me into his mouth and began to suck.

I let out a moan and felt my knees would've buckled if we weren't already kneeling, as his lips closed around me and I was buried inside that warm wet cavern of his mouth. My cock felt like it swelled even further to fill the vacuum created by his suction. His tongue began to rub the underside of the shaft, without letting his lips lose their lock around the base of my cock. For a moment, I tried to figure out if he were impaled upon my cock, or if I was the one who'd been captured by his lips, but I didn't really care it felt so good. I could feel him swallow, the slick muscles at the back of his throat tightening and squirming around my thick tool, and he tried to take even more of me into himself, even though his nose was pressed flat against my belly and his lips were closed on that part of my shaft where the pubic hair crept onto the first half inch. There was no place for him to go, so he just sucked even harder; I had to wonder how he could breathe like that. I would've hit my gag reflex long ago.

But it felt so good, and he didn't seem to have any problems breathing, so I stopped worrying about him and grabbed his hair. I broke the lock on his lips by pushing his head from me and pulling part-way out of his mouth, only to thrust my way back down his wet throat a moment later.

Without warning, Phil spat out my cock.

"And where do you think you're going?" I asked him, grabbing my dick in one hand and pumping myself with the lube from his saliva. It felt good to squeeze my cock more tightly than his lips could, but nothing like being surrounded by a fat wet tongue and mouth.

Phil didn't answer. He turned from me and pulled a condom and a small bottle of lube from his backpack.

"You were planning this all along, weren't you?" I asked.

Again, Phil didn't answer, just smiled and unrolled the condom over my cock. I should've realized Phil would see any excursion as a new, unusual location in which to have sex. I took the bottle of lube from him and poured a dollop onto my finger as he turned around and thrust his ass up to me again, bracing himself with a branch of the ornamental pear tree we were standing beneath. I rubbed the lube over his puckered hole, already loosened by my tonguing, and then coated my finger with the viscous gel, rubbing it up and down along his crack where the lube clung, matting down the dark hairs. As I pressed my finger directly on the roseate bud of his asshole and began to massage it in a tight circle, I couldn't help thinking of it being like one of the stained-glass rose windows so common in Christian architecture, including the cloisters around us.

Phil was in no mood for theological or architectural musings, however, and pushed backward against my finger. I slid into his ass up to my second knuckle where the finger widened, then began twisting my hand like a corkscrew as I pushed deeper into him. "You know why unicorns only like virgins?" I asked him.

Phil broke off moaning long enough to ask, "No, why?" as I twisted inside him. I pulled my fingers out so he could concentrate on my answer, and held the base of my cock against his hole as I prepared to reply.

"Because they like a tight piece of ass," I answered, and sunk into him. I fucked him in long slow strokes at first, getting him used to my thick cock being inside of him before beginning to increase the pace.

"If you're the unicorn," Phil asked me as I pumped into him, "how come I'm the one being ridden?"

"Just shut up and enjoy the ride," I answered. "Or I'll stop." I paused, half out of him, for emphasis, as if I could actually call things off right now without getting the worst case of blueballs I could imagine.

"Don't you dare," he said and reached back to grab my hips and pull me deeper into him. "Giddyap already."

I giddyapped, thrusting into him faster and faster. He was jerking himself off in time to my pumping. I was always jealous of the fact that he could get hard again so quickly after coming. I took forever to build to an orgasm, and once I had I was out of commission for a good while. Which made for some agonizingly pleasurable nights, since Phil loved trying to coax me into getting hard again right after I'd come.

I could feel myself on the verge, though, as if I were about to break into a gallop, I was tearing into Phil's ass so fast. My back broke a fresh sweat. I could smell the sweet scent of Phil's cum still lingering in the air, from when he'd shot all over the wall, and thinking about eating him out again pushed me over into release. My cock spasmed inside him, squirting load after load of hot jism into the condom's reservoir tip. At last I came to a stop, my cock still buried deep inside him, and half-collapsed against him, trying to catch my breath. Phil began to beat himself off again while I was still within him, and a moment later he cried out and shot a second barrage of jism against the cloister wall.

"So this is why unicorns are so magical," Phil said as I pulled out of him. I slid the condom from my cock and tied a knot in it to keep the jism from spilling out. "A far cry from just a horse with a horn, I say." He handed me tissues from his backpack and wiped himself off before zipping up his pants.

"Next week we can go to the Claremont Stables on Amsterdam and 82nd," I said, pulling up my own jeans and looking about the still-empty courtyard, "see if we can't frighten the mundane horses."

Clothes Make the Man

George's apartment was a bizarre tableau of half-dressed fags. George designed porn CD-ROMs for a living, but this wasn't a shoot for his latest title. In one of the previous jobs on his long and checkered resumé he'd been a mannequin designer, and it was for that reason ten gay boys had descended upon his apartment like a plague of locusts before the harvest. When the mannequin company folded, George had been left with more than a hundred wigs in his possession, and while he'd lost or given away many of them over the years, he still had at least sixty left. Every year about a dozen fags would show up on his doorstep on Wigstock morning (and also Halloween) begging to borrow a wig and be made-up.

Now, I've always found partial clothing to be extremely sexy. A man in a vest with no shirt on underneath will wind up inadvertently giving you a flash of nipple every now and then, and soon you find yourself waiting for it, watching for it, because it's so unexpected when the drape of fabric will suddenly fall back to reveal that pert brown circle. Or as your lover walks unabashedly about the apartment you share wearing only silk boxers, your eyes keep falling to the fly as it gapes and yawns and gives you a flash of the dark hair beneath and—what you're really hungering for—a glimpse of cock, momentary, like a flashbulb on a camera, and like that brilliant light it lingers on your vision even after fading away.

There's something about men who are partially dressed in women's clothing (especially butch men like the Chelsea gym queens now before me) that's even more attractive, because it accentuates their masculinity. For instance, Bernie (short for Bernardo) was one of those deceptive Italian studs—all muscle and meat on the outside, but such a soft and nelly voice the moment he opens his mouth, seemingly so out of character with the rest of him. But right now he had his mouth quite closed as he puckered his lipsticked lips and, shirtless, postured in front of the full-body mirror on the closet door in a pair of silver elbow-length gloves. He put his hands on his hips and pouted into the mirror, trying on different expressions.

I marveled at the intense musculature of his back, the way his shoulders and biceps faded into those slender-seeming gloves, the way his top-heavy torso faded into his Calvin Klein boxer-briefs, which poked out from beneath his practically non-existent cut-offs. He had a firm, round ass, and his legs were undeniably male: thick columns of muscle. I imagined them wrapped around me and squeezing tightly, and me being unable to move, pinned by their strength and bulk.

Bernie caught my eye in the mirror and said, "Honey, you're going to need to tuck that thing." He stepped aside and I got a look at myself in the mirror and blushed. I was wearing an orange and yellow dress that looked like it had once been the wallpaper on Continental Airlines back in the '70s, and I had an erection tenting it out in front of me from watching him and fantasizing.

I strutted forward, wobbling a bit in my heels in part for effect and in part because I didn't really know how to walk properly yet. I stood right behind him, and rubbed my crotch against his ass. "You want me to tuck it in here, did you say?"

I got whistles and hoots of laughter from the other boys, who'd paused in their own preparations to pay attention to this latest mini-drama. Or maybe they'd all stopped to check out my basket. I stepped beside Bernie and stared at myself next to him. How could I properly cruise any of these boys when they couldn't see how my body really was? My best friend (who was to be called Royal Flush today) and I were at George's before any of them, and my make-up was well under way by the time anyone else arrived. I was done up to look like Agnes Moorhead as Endora from "Bewitched," with bright orange lipstick and blue and purple eyeshadow on thick. George had done wonders, but that was always the case with him. He had one of those senses of style that could create art—or camp—out of anything or anyone.

I wore chunky plastic rings in various loud colors that matched or accentuated the dress, and plastic yellow bangles. A string of yellow pearls was wrapped twice around my neck like a choker. My wig was sitting on a mannequin head atop the television: Elizabeth Taylor big hair, the same color as my own so I didn't need to worry about the back of my own hair showing through at the bottom of the wig in a little dovetail. All I had left to do were my nails, in a garish orange glitter I'd found for a buck fifty that morning at the corner drug store.

George's latest CD-ROM was playing on the computer behind me, and everyone was ragging him over the dialogue and the script and the performers he'd cast. Eric sat at the keyboard, controlling the action.

"This one's balls look deformed, George—couldn't you have found someone who looks more normal?"

"His cock is big and that's all that matters in these things."

"That's right, it's only when you've got a little dick that you need to have a perfect body and face."

I couldn't keep track of who was talking, but it didn't really matter; the overall effect was what was important. I knew George from before today but had only just met all the rest of the boys, except of course for Royal Flush. And also Jordan, who was the boyfriend of one of George's friends and had been the boyfriend of someone I knew at college. There were a few boys I'd been able to pin names to, but I quickly forgot most of them as soon as I was introduced. Half the boys seemed to know each other from before, although I couldn't tell if they were friends or just remembered each other from George's apartment last Wigstock. I saw at least two boys exchange phone numbers, and there was certainly a fair amount of cruising going on, especially as guys took off certain particles of clothes to struggle into dresses.

I had had my eye set on a boy named Nathan since the moment he walked in. Right now, he was just sitting on the couch, watching it all happen around him, and there was something about the demure way he sat that really turned me on. That semi-overwhelmed look made him seem so wholesome, like a Midwestern tourist on his first visit to New York, and in some way it made him seem young, even though I thought he was probably three or four years older than I was, maybe twenty-eight, twenty-nine. Which was a bit young for how I usually like my men, when I want a relationship, but just fine for some hot and sweaty, guiltless sex.

Nathan was wearing a very slutty clubbing shirt, very East Village, an all-white sequin crop top with a wide collar and a zipper down to his navel, but all very much a boy's cut. He wasn't planning on wearing a dress today, just a wig. Half the boys, it turned out, were doing demi-drag, although they were having fun trying on various dresses while they were getting ready and using it as an excuse to strut their stuff for each other. Nathan had found a little blond bob, like Marilyn Monroe in "Some Like It Hot," which suited him quite well.

I didn't know him and I didn't know the couple he'd come here with, but as an excuse to start talking with him I took the bottle of orange nail polish that worked so fabulously with my equally-garish dress, sat down next to him on the couch, and stared into his eyes while I asked him, fluttering my mascara-ed eyelashes and trying to sound forced-innocent as I held the bottle out to him, if he would do me.

He gave me the once over, unmistakably undressing me in his mind, having caught the obvious double entendre. I felt even more turned on than I usually did when I knew someone was checking me out, because I knew he was able to see the male me beneath the dress. And also because I knew my body was different because of the drag: I'd shaved. Chest, legs, armpits, all smooth flesh. Soon I'd have stubble all over my body, coarse and prickly, rubbing against the inside of my clothes, rubbing against other flesh. I tried to imagine how it would feel to run a tongue across my stubbly chest and nipples. This decision I'd made—to do drag for Wigstock with my friend—was going to be with me for many weeks.

My friend, Miss Flush, was a swimmer, and had even taken a medal at the Gay Games last year. I remembered the stories she'd told me (her make-up was done now and she had her wig on, so her gender had changed over when we talked about her, same as mine had since I was also mostly done except for the nails and wig) about shaving down before the meets, how everyone was checking each other out as they shaved each others' nearly-naked bodies, how it was all intensely erotic, male flesh everywhere, bulging out of tiny Speedos. The scene here was kind of like that, with everything serving to remind you that these bodies were so male underneath the make-up and the wigs, underneath the shaved chests and armpits and legs.

I'd never done drag before, except once during my freshman year in high school when I played Juliette in a skit we performed at a pep rally. As the youngest member of the track team, I was given the most humiliating part. And because I had that lanky young boy runner's frame I looked much more femme than any of the women, who were all rather square-shouldered and thick-calved from running and working out for years.

"Sure," Nathan said, taking the bottle of polish from me.

The phone rang. George picked it up and said, "Salon."

I looked over my shoulder to watch the computer screen for a moment. They were picking strippers, and a not-especially-attractive skinhead with a big dick was beating himself off on the black leather couch that Nathan and I were now sitting on. I tried to imagine this apartment as the set of a porn shoot. One way to cut costs.

"Look at this," Eric was saying, "the leather guy just said he was 25 in the sound byte, but his statistics say he's 29."

"Can't we watch the guppie sequence again?" Bernie begged.

"Look at how long his nails are," Peter exclaimed, as the action moved in for a close-up of the guy fisting his meat just before the cum shot.

I looked down at my own nails. Nathan was working on my third one, painting with even strokes from the moon toward the tip. I couldn't help glancing down past our cluster of fingers into his crotch, so near at hand, as it were, and looking oh so inviting.

"Flo has such lovely long fingers," Nathan said, lifting my hand for a moment to show everyone his handiwork at painting my nails, then replacing my hand on his knee. "I bet they'd feel great wrapped around a cock."

He didn't look up as he said this, but continued to paint the next nail. It was the same sort of machismo semi-porn talk we'd all been making all afternoon, so I didn't really think he meant for me to act on it. It was all bravado. But I wanted to take him up on it so badly, and I wondered what he'd do if I called his bluff. He was flirting with me, I knew, which felt great since I was so unsure how I looked right then. I'm not usually much of an exhibitionist, but then, I don't usually wear a dress; maybe there was something about already being so far out there in terms of my appearance that made me bolder than normal.

"That can be easily arranged," I said, and with my free hand I unzipped his jeans. My fingers snaked into his fly and worked their way across his underwear, groping along his cock and balls. I could feel him begin to stiffen under my touch, through the fabric. He was wearing white briefs of some sort, and I tugged at the elastic waistband to free his cock. I pulled it through the fly of his jeans, as it continued to swell within my hand, and began working my way up and down the shaft.

Around us, everyone was going about their business as usual. The phone rang and George answered it, "Futura Bold."

Simon declared, "Looks like we've lost two queens before we've even started."

But once they got a look at Nathan's prick they went back to their own preparations.

Except for Bernie.

Bernie was digging about in the cardboard box of wigs and a moment later came striding over to us with a long blonde braid that was meant as an extension. "I always knew you were a bottle job," Bernie told Nathan as he wrapped the extension around Nathan's cock and balls, tying it off with a flourish and a bow. "There now," he said, "crotch-wig-slash-cock-ring," and turned on his heels away from us.

I was still pumping up and down on Nathan's cock as he painted a second coat on the nails of my left hand. His strokes were no longer as even as they had been, but he was trying.

"So, how do they feel?" I asked him, squeezing as I brought my hand down towards his balls.

"Good," he said, his voice cracking a little, unexpectedly, as his breath caught.

I smiled. "Good. Now, blow on these until they dry," I said, holding my hand in front of his face as if I intended for him to kiss it, "while I blow on this."

I slid off the couch and with my free hand pulled my dress under me as I crouched between his knees. He gripped my left wrist with both his hands, and his stiff cock jerked in anticipation. I wanted it down my throat, but I was going to tease him until his balls ached. I leaned forward and kissed the head, all lip, leaving the imprint of an orange lipstick crown.

The phone rang and George answered it, "Helvetica Black." The doorbell rang simultaneously.

My heart began to pound as I was reminded that I was having sex in public like this, in front of total strangers. With a total stranger, for that matter, although that didn't bother me. Not knowing the onlookers, however, especially not knowing who just came in or how they would react, did disturb me. Sure, most of the guys weren't watching us all the time, and they weren't watching us with the intention of getting off from watching us, but they certainly looked over at us from time to time, curious if nothing else. I wondered what they were thinking. They hadn't exactly voiced their acceptance of Nathan and me having sex in front of them, but they hadn't withheld their consent either. The newcomers hadn't yet had a chance to withhold their consent. As my face hovered in front of Nathan's eagerly twitching cock, I wondered what to do and how they would respond, while a zillion other hang-ups and concerns held me frozen with indecision.

Then I remembered that for today I was a bitchy, irreverent drag queen and I opened my mouth. My tongue met the warm, dry flesh of Nathan's cock and eagerly began bathing it in saliva, wetting it down for my orange lips to glide smoothly along the shaft. With my right hand, I grabbed the base of his cock and pulled it toward me, positioning it. My lips sunk lower, toward the blond braid that Bernie had tied on. I rocked back and forth on my high heels, his cock sliding into and out of my mouth with the motion.

My own cock was throbbing insistently beneath my dress. With my right hand (I still didn't trust that the nails of my left were dry) I reached beneath the folds of fabric to grab hold of it, poking out from my loose boxer shorts. I began to jerk off, thrusting into my palm each time I rocked forward onto Nathan's cock.

My knees began to ache, and I stood up. I felt like I'd been doing squats at the gym for two hours solid. "Now, don't you move," I told Nathan. He twitched his cock. "Well, *you* can move," I conceded, pointing at it.

I reached beside him on the couch for my clutch purse and opened it. I pulled out a condom. "A girl's got to be prepared," I said, and tore it open with my teeth.

Before I had a chance to roll it over Nathan's cock, however, Nathan lifted up the skirt of my dress and tugged down my boxer shorts. He pulled me toward him, and his mouth closed about my dick as he eagerly shoved himself onto me.

"I told you not to move," I complained, although I didn't mean a word of it. I wanted him to move and keep moving, his mouth sliding up and down along my dick, his pointed tongue probing into the loose folds of my ballsac as my entire shaft was in his mouth, or swirling around the crown when he pulled back.

The couple who had come in when the doorbell rang—a towheaded blond and his dark-skinned Brazilian-looking lover—was staring at us, curious and unbelieving and semi-uncomfortable by such blatant sexuality. They looked away when our eyes met. I didn't care, let them watch. My skirt had dropped over Nathan's head, so all they could see was the bobbing orange fabric, anyway. All I could see was bobbing orange fabric, too, but damned if it didn't feel fine.

Nathan pulled off my cock for air, lying back against the couch as he caught his breath. One hand still held his own cock, which he'd been tugging on as he sucked me off. His dick was bright red, swollen from his desire and the crotch-wig-slash-cock-ring. I delicately stepped out of my boxer shorts, which I realized were foolish things to be wearing when I was in drag and would need to "tuck." The unrolled condom in my hand had begun to go dry, but I had a small bottle of lube in my clutch purse. "A girl's got to be prepared," I said again as I knelt down in front of Nathan with the lube in one hand and the condom in the other.

I greased his dick and rolled the condom onto it. "Hold this," I said and lifted my skirt. Nathan held the edge of the fabric for me, and I lubed my ass quickly, slicking my hole down for easy, painless access. I squirted some more lube onto his condomed cock for good measure, and then straddled him. He was still holding my skirt up, as if he were a voyeur peeking under my dress to see my genitals. That turned me on. Slowly, I lowered myself onto him, positioning his cock with my hands.

It is always a curious feeling, I think, to have a man's cock inside your body. No matter how much I want it, my body still resists, at least a little bit. I wrestled with myself—I want this cock inside me NOW—and tried to relax. He was in, but something was not right yet. I shifted, I adjusted, I breathed deeply. His cock felt good in there, I felt good. I flexed my legs, lifting myself off him slightly, and then slid back down. I was in control. Nathan lay on the couch as I fucked myself on his cock, holding my skirt up so he could watch what was happening, the inches of his cock disappearing up my ass.

I felt I was getting near to coming as I rode his cock. I settled onto him and stopped for a moment, resting, delaying the moment of orgasm to draw out this delicious feeling of sex for as long as possible. We didn't move, but we changed roles. He took charge. I unzipped his sequined crop top. His stomach beneath was pale, with a small thatch of hair on his chest. The sides of the shirt fell back as his body shifted on the couch, thrusting his cock up into me. I tweaked his now-exposed nipples, but soon abandoned them to lift my dress. Again, I felt a delicious exhibitionistic thrill as I held the skirt aloft. It felt so dirty, like I was flashing him, and I think that feeling turned me on even more than the fact of our flesh sliding together.

I was bouncing up and down on his cock, holding the dress away from my cock, which flopped rhythmically against his abs. And then my cock spasmed and I was cumming, orgasm rolling through my entire body in quick shudders. Four of them, then a long sigh.

My cum shined on Nathan's chest like melted white sequins. His cock was still inside me, and once I caught my breath he continued to thrust up into me. I leaned forward and rolled his nipples between my fingers again, urging him on toward climax. Suddenly I tugged on them, hard. Nathan cried out and began to cum. I clenched my ass, holding onto him tightly as his cock squirmed within me, shooting his cum into the condom's reservoir tip.

When he lay still, pleasantly spent from his orgasm, I grabbed my purse, which lay beside him on the couch. His cock was still comfortably inside me as it began to go soft. I took out my lipstick and, using the mirror in my compact, touched up my make-up. When I was satisfied, I leaned forward and left a perfect lipstick mark above his right nipple.

Nathan smiled, dreamily, and started to sit up, to disentangle his body from mine, where we were still joined together under my skirt. I pushed him back down on the couch. "Where do you think you're going?" I asked him, and handed him the bottle of orange glitter polish. "You've still got to take care of my other hand."

The Story of Eau

Our kitchen table is a once-elegant claw-foot porcelain bathtub nearly as old as the building, with an inch-and-a-half-thick slab of oak laid on top of it. The tub is wonderfully deep; in my last apartment, up in Hell's Kitchen, I had a normal tub: which is to say, both too short and too shallow. While my current tub in the East Village apartment I share with my lover, Tim, is still on the short side for someone like myself who stands on the far side of six feet, it compensates by being deep enough that my knees don't stick out into the cool air when I sit in it, as they have in almost all my previous tubs. It was perfect for sitting in for long stretches of time, relaxing and reading—provided one wasn't fussy about maybe getting the pages wet. But ever since my doctor ordered me to take two or three sitz baths each day to cure my hemorrhoids, I've had better things to do in the tub than read.

You might not think that getting hemorrhoids could improve the sex life of a balding thirtysomething-year-old gay man living in Manhattan, but then you don't know my lover, Tim. (If you're one of his ex-lovers, then you're lucky enough to know what I mean. But I'm the luckiest of all, since I'm the one who has him now. Knock wood.)

In order to encourage me to follow doctor's orders and take

all of the prescribed daily baths, Tim has taken it upon himself to create a little bathing ritual to pamper me. I tease him sometimes that his tender ministrations are really motivated by self-interest, since the sooner I'm healed, the sooner it'll be that he can fuck me again. But I have a feeling that even after I'm well, we'll continue our little bathing rituals (although probably *not* two or three times per day!)

We used to take baths only rarely, and not just because the bathtub was in the kitchen and also used as our dining table, which meant it was always covered in stuff, from dirty dishes to piles of bills. Admittedly, it required a concerted effort to decide to take a bath, since one had to first clean off the kitchen table, then remove the heavy table top. But even the effort and time-lag of running the bathwater took far too long and was too much trouble for the pace of life in New York City, let alone the extra hassle. It was a luxury we never seemed to have time for, or didn't often allow ourselves to take even when we did have the time. We had a shower in a tiny closet, and a toilet in a closet of its own right next to it, both of which also stood in the large kitchen that the apartment's front door opened into. East Village apartments are like that, sort of hobbled together after the fact, instead of having been designed to be a living space. But they were cheaper than just about anywhere else in New York City, and necessity made a lot of things worth putting up with.

Our little bathing rituals developed because one of the first times I took one of my post-doctor's-visit baths, Tim was home watching me. You'd think that after all the trouble of running a bath, I'd sit in it for a while. But I felt foolish, especially when I thought about why I was doing what I was doing and thinking it would never really work. Of course, negative thinking is the worst thing one can do in one of these alternative therapies, but that's what I was thinking, and that sort of thinking is what made me stand up after about four minutes.

Tim would have none of that, though. "Where do you think you're going?" he asked me. "I'm done with my bath," I said lamely. "Not yet, you're not," Tim said, "now sit down," and I did, as he disappeared into the bedroom. He came back a moment later with something behind his back. He stood behind me and I leaned my head back against the rim of the tub to look up at him. He smiled down at me and ran one hand along my torso and neck, leaning forward so he could kiss me. His other hand was still behind his back and I wondered what he held there, but then I closed my eyes and thought only of our tongues and our mouths until we paused to each catch our breath. I let my arms dangle over the sides, my head resting against the lip of the tub, my eyes still closed as I soaked in the warm water, and I thought "this is nice" and felt my body suddenly lose its tenseness, everything opening up, even my anus, which felt almost like a fist unclosing, with that sense of relief you feel after you let go of anger.

It was at that moment that I learned what Tim had been holding behind his back—handcuffs, which clicked around my wrist and one clawed foot. "You fink!" I cried at Tim, although I didn't open my eyes. I didn't want to move from the warm place I was in, both the bath and the afterglow of our kiss, which had kickstarted my arousal. Maybe that was part of the warmth, I thought, the flush of blood rushing through my body to fill my cock. With my eyes still shut, I felt the cold metal loop around my wrist and said to Tim, "I want another kiss."

He didn't answer, but a moment later I felt his presence behind me again, his body close, and then his fingers were touching my chest and neck, caressing my throat as they moved to float lightly over my lips. His breath followed next, warm and fragrant of the vanilla-pear tea he'd been drinking after dinner, his lips hesitating a hair's breadth away from mine. My tongue poked out to lick at him real quick and I said "Ribbit" and we both laughed. And then we were breathing the same breath again, our mouths sealed tightly to one another as he held my chin in his hands and our tongues tried to wrap themselves around each other. One of the first things that made me fall in love with Tim is how well he kisses, how it makes you feel there's nothing in the world he wants to do in that moment except kiss you, that he hasn't another thought in his head. So many men I've kissed not only lack the talent or the natural advantage of Tim's thick pliant lips, but you can tell their mind's not in it—they're worrying about whether they left the oven on or what bills need to be paid before next week or whether your kiss will turn out to be the beginning of an ongoing romance or a one-night stand or perhaps just a kiss. Tim's kisses could make me forget the worst of days at work and think only of him and our romance, and his agile tongue sent waves of sexual energy coursing through me.

"I thought I was supposed to relax," I complained when we broke apart and I'd caught my breath. I lifted my hips so that my erection poked out of the tub like the periscope of a surfacing submarine, its blind eye looking at Tim.

I waited for his reaction, wondering if he would just leave me like this. I was at his mercy, after all; even aside from the bath, I was still cuffed to the tub, with the keys still in the bedroom, for all I knew.

Tim smiled and dipped a hand into the warm water to slide up and down my inner thighs. I relaxed my hips and sunk back to the bottom of the tub. Tim's fingers kept stroking and poking along my legs and crotch and balls, before dropping down to hover near my tender asshole. "You're supposed to relax here," he said gently, his poking fingers as soft in their touch as the tone of his voice. His other hand plunged into the water and grabbed my cock as he said, "But that doesn't mean we can't get a little excited elsewhere."

My entire body tensed. He just held my cock in his fist, as his first hand poked at my asshole again. "Relax," he commanded, and I let my breath go and tried to follow his command, again imagining my asshole opening like an unclenching fist. "Much better," Tim said and started gently stroking my cock with his other hand. The motion created small waves that made my balls bounce; it felt like warm mouths sucking at all the skin of my groin at once.

"Much better," I agreed, closing my eyes again as I leaned back and purred while one of Tim's hands moved on my cock and the other gently probed my ass. I could feel a bead of pre-cum building and I squeezed once to send it shooting out, wondering whether it would float to the surface or just sit at the tip of my cock.

Tim's hands stopped moving. "What?" I asked, opening my eyes.

He explained, "If you don't stay relaxed here" and his fingers swirled along the crack between my cheeks for emphasis, "I stop moving here," and again his fingers danced for emphasis, this time swirling around the underside of the crown where he knew I was most sensitive. My back arched instinctively as his fingers rubbed along there, and I knew I was starting to clench my asshole again, but I stopped myself, breathed out, and focused on keeping my asshole as open as possible. The pleasure in my cock kept building as his hand swirled around the glans.

"That's my boy," Tim said, and after a moment more he let me relax, sliding his hand down onto the shaft and beginning to pump, the change in stroke allowing me to catch my breath and adjust to the new, differently pleasurable sensation. Tim knew my body well, and knew how to work me, turning me on until I was about to crest over into orgasm and then changing his grip to delay things, over and over again, until at last I couldn't hold back any longer.

"I'm going to come," I warned him. "I'm going to clench, and don't you dare stop!"

Tim didn't stop and a few seconds later my hips were bucking as I came, my dick spewing above the rippling water like a whale's blowhole spray.

My orgasm had splashed water all over the place. I looked over at Tim, who stood by the tub, his shirt and pants clinging to him. With my free hand, I reached across myself and started rubbing his hard cock where its outline showed through the wet fabric of his pants. I hooked my fingers behind his belt buckle and pulled him toward me, since my reach wasn't very good given the awkward position I was in.

"I think my bath is done for tonight, don't you agree?" I said, tugging on my anchored arm until the cuffs clanked against the porcelain tub. "I think this'll feel much better for both of us if you let me loose again."

Tim looked down at me with a gleam in his eye as if he were thinking of leaving me chained there for good. My fingers squeezed his cock tight, and then I let go of him, settling back in the tub as if I were completely unaware of his presence. Tim hesitated a moment longer, looking down at me in the tub as I tried my best not to look up at him or crack up laughing, before he headed into the bedroom without a word. He let me stew a good while, wondering if he planned to spring me after all, whether he'd gone to bed, if he'd lost the key. But eventually he returned, sans his wet clothes, but with the key to the handcuffs.

His cock had begun to soften from the state it had been in under his wet clothes, but it was still half-hard. It throbbed slightly as the blood pumped through it as he stood beside the tub. He held the key up and my eyes shifted from his genitals to his hands. "You want out," he began, making his dick give a jump as he flexed that muscle in the perineum that I was supposed to be relaxing, calling my attention to his crotch again. I didn't need any further encouragement and eagerly opened my mouth to earn my release—and his.

And thus began the bathing rituals.

The rituals vary, depending on the time of day. Night-time baths are more elaborate, which isn't any great surprise since both of us have more time then and less pressures from the world outside our little apartment. But there are certain other intrinsic factors that lend themselves to this sort of extra elaboration at night, like lighting. By day, there's really not much you can do, one way or the other, to create a mood or atmosphere with lighting, but for our nightly baths, Tim has bought these enormous three-wick scented candles, which he'll place on the windowsill or the stovetop or the floor. They cast a soft, flickering light and perfume the air with their aromatic essences—vanilla, lavender, jasmine—all of which help cast a quiet, romantic overtone to what we're about to enact, the perfect ambiance in which to relax into each other's love and caring and our mutual desire. Sometimes, when Tim is feeling playful, he'll make shadow animals with his hands and cast them against the far wall, the porcelain's tub, my flesh beneath the water's ripples. His favorite is to cast a wolf's head and have it stalk across my body until the image snaps at my cock beneath the water. Depending on Tim's mood, the Shadow Wolf either tries to bite it off or perform fellatio.

If we're eating at home, the night ritual starts with dinner.

But even if we're dining out, our repast plays a healthy part in the healing, since I've had to cut back on certain foods that can irritate the hemorrhoids. Thai is pretty much verboten for now, since all my favorite foods are either spicy or have nuts, and Indian and Korean have likewise proven too rough on my sensitive system. Also forbidden is my after-work Snickers bar while waiting for the subway. One of the advantages of living in New York City is that we've got every type of cuisine from around the world, so there are still plenty of savory options I'm allowed. Most of the time we eat at home anyway, not just because it saves money but because both Tim and I love to cook.

It doesn't matter whether Tim or I am preparing dinner, it's all part of the ritual. We're beyond the score-keeping stage of the relationship and simply relish in the nourishment of feeding and our pleasure in eating—and the other pleasures that are to come.

Sometimes, while we're cooking, Tim will slide the table-top a few inches and begin running a bath. The wood lid serves to keep the water hot, and as we eat, the tub radiates warmth to our legs. It's a delicious feeling that starts the relaxation as tension begins to drain from our legs and drip away through the soles of the feet. Because New York is such a pedestrian town, we're all of us on our feet all day long, dealing with the hassles of commuting and crowds and worrying about being late and in general just pounding the pavement.

And once the food starts to hit the stomach, satisfying both hunger and taste buds, it's so much easier to let go of all that stored-up tension and worry from the day. Which is what made the rituals as important as the baths themselves; they removed, or at least dealt with, some of the possible causes of the hemorrhoids in the first place. They were an attention to the details of daily pleasures in our lives, all those small sensory moments of joy that we so often overlook or don't consider significant. And the most important part of the rituals, the togetherness, is the truest panacea that exists.

All of those small details, more than the sex we had before, during, or after I slid into the warm water, was what came to matter most to us. Sex was just one of the ways we expressed our delight in each other, that giving of pleasure and the receiving of it in return.

Mind you, we like the sex a lot too, wet and messy as it often becomes. Night-time baths always begin slow and gentle, with Tim and I taking turns using a sponge across each other's bodies. We've bought water toys for each other: rubber duckies and funny soaps and wind-up plastic frogs that kick their legs and swim. I bought a little catnip mouse the day after Tim bought me a small boat, and we played Stuart Little for a while until our playing with each other knocked the mouse and boat out of the tub. Sometimes Tim would join me in the tub, sometimes he'd stand outside it, naked by my side. Either way, we'd usually wind up splashing water all over the linoleum by the time we were done for the night and moved into the bedroom to drift into sleep or the living room for some mindless television viewing while we cuddled.

The daytime baths have their rituals as well, although neither of us can really afford to take as much time with them because of our jobs. But the whole act of this enforced relaxation has made both of us aware of how much daily stress we had in our life, from jobs to socializing to just getting through the day, and how much of it was self-imposed. Taking time out to interrupt our hectic schedules has been proof positive that we can stop to smell the roses, as it were, and calm down and still accomplish everything important that we need to.

Often, when we are on tight schedules at work and can't afford to run over time, Tim will come home on his lunch break a half hour before me. He'll cook something for us to eat and begin to draw a bath for me. By the time I get home, he has eaten already. I am ordered right into the tub, and it is only when Tim has to head back to work that I'm allowed to get up and dry off and get dressed again. I am also permitted to eat whatever Tim had cooked up for me.

It was hard, sometimes, to relax for these lunch-time trysts, when we always had to keep one eye on the clock. But at the same time, it was invigorating. There was something both romantic and illicit about having a "nooner"—quick sex in the afternoon before going back to work—and I think both of us tackled our afternoon's tasks with more pep as a result.

For day-time baths, Tim didn't fill the tub entirely. I'd already showered in the morning, and the important part of my anatomy, as far as these baths were concerned, was my ass; with only a few inches of water in the tub, my sore ass was sure to stay covered.

Of course, before any bathing—night or day—there is the undressing. No matter how pressured we were to get back to work, undressing me was one thing Tim never rushed. Often, during the day, I was not allowed to undress Tim in turn, since we didn't have the time for sex or we had to be careful to keep him from getting wet. Sometimes I'd unzip his fly despite his protests, and suck his cock while I soaked my rear. We didn't always climax during these daytime baths, that wasn't the point. And Tim never seemed to tire of making me feel like he truly cared that I was healing, that he was an active part of the cure. I'm sure that if anything helped me get better, his love was the medicine that did it as much as the baths, that focus and atten- tion he paid my body as he slowly pulled a sock from my foot, holding my leg with his other hand to support it as the sock came free, and lowering my leg gently back to the ground until I could put weight on it and support myself again.

At night, we had the time to peel each other from our clothes, and it was like pulling away all the cares and worries of the outside world, until only the two of us remained, stripped down to the essence of our being and our relationship, our skin raw with desire for one another other. And we kiss and embrace and caress one another, and our movements send candle-lit shadows flickering, and whirls of steam rise from the porcelain claw-foot tub in our kitchen.

And to think that when I was a kid, I used to live in terror of one of my parents saying those two most-feared words, "Bath Time!" Oh, what a world of difference being in love makes!

Water Taxi

The rough orange fabric of the life jacket was rubbing my nipples raw. At times like this I'm glad I didn't let Jaume talk me into getting my nipple pierced when he had his done. I like the way it looks, the small silver loop, especially since he only had one side pierced; I don't know, when men have both sides done it makes me think of door knockers, and the whole aesthetic changes and loses something. But I thought he must be suffering more from the life preserver than I was right now, since the pierced tit is supposed to be more sensitive than before.

Jaume, though, didn't seem about to complain. He sat at the prow of the double kayak, his powerful arms dipping to one side and then the other as he paddled. His shoulders were hidden under the life preserver, but I could watch the musculature of his back flex as he twisted left and right with each stroke, and I wondered once again what I'd done to be so lucky to have such a beautiful man as my boyfriend. I felt lucky about everything right then—Jaume, the crystal-clear blue sky, the afternoon sun, the warm surf, the party on the beach, life in general. I forgot about my sore nipples and matched Jaume's strokes, and we just glided across the waves for a while.

Neither of us had used a kayak before, and thus when the DJ

announced free kayaks as part of this year's Gay Pride Festival on the beach, Jaume and I jumped up from our beach towels and trotted over to the launch area. This was the first year that Barcelona held a Gay Pride Festival at the beach, with an afternoon full of activities like volleyball games, while speakers blared dance music. Later in the evening, we'd all move into the Pabellon del Mar behind us for a long night of performances by bands like Baccara and Folkloricas Arrepentidas, and drag shows by Arroba and other queens I'd never heard of. And, of course, normal club dance music in between all that. It was expected that many men would come just for the dance. Half the money from the entrance fee would go to the fight against AIDS, so there was a serious side to the festivities as well.

I wondered if it would work. The gay political groups of Barcelona were always fighting with each other, and this year they'd split off, with one group having a Gay Pride march on June 28th, commemorating the Stonewall Revolution back in the U.S. that started the modern homosexual rights movement. The other half, including most of the owners of the gay businesses, decided to hold a more festive event on Sunday, July 4th, to try to get a better turnout. It was Independence Day in the States, they joked, and they were breaking free of the U.S. domination of gay culture in other parts of the world. After all, they said, why should we celebrate an American Gay Pride holiday instead of creating one of our own?

I sometimes feel guilty that I'm not more politically active, but the truth of the matter is, I'm easily bored by such things. I know it's important to vote, and I do, but I just can't stand the endless squabbling at meetings over which subgroup feels they're not getting enough representation and so on. I mean, I'm glad there are dedicated activists out there who understand the legal jargon better than I and know how to play the system —who are fighting for my right to kiss my boyfriend on the beach like I did a few minutes ago. Like many of the guys on the beach today, I'm sure, Jaume and I were just here to have fun. We went to the march on Monday to show our support and help boost the numbers—now that the groups were split up we figured it would be especially important to put in an appearance—and we also came to the fun-in-the-sun party.

My mind was wandering as my body worked through the simple repetitive task of kayaking, but I was awakened from these musings by a call from a pleasure boat that had anchored in front of the beach, neither especially near to nor all that far out from the shore, as if undecided whether they wanted to simply watch the festivities or be included. Apart from the all-male crew on the deck, it was obvious from even a cursory glance at their postures as they stood about drinking afternoon cocktails and watching the shore that they were not here by mistake but had come for the Gay Pride party.

One of the men, blond and shirtless, was leaning over the side and hailing us. I was sure it was us because when he saw us glance up he waved in our direction, but I looked over my shoulder anyway. I had that feeling like when you're in a crowded bar and a guy you think is cute smiles at you, and you can't believe he's really smiling at you, certain that one of his friends or some hot number must be standing just behind your shoulder and is in fact the intended recipient of the smile.

"What do you think?" Jaume asked, not breaking his stroke. We were angling parallel to the beach, and if their boat had been in motion our paths would've crossed in a hundred meters or so.

"Why not see what he wants?" I answered, using my paddle to change our course. "Maybe they want to offer us a drink?" I laughed and our little shared kayak spun around toward the boat, and in a moment I again matched Jaume's even strokes.

As we drew up to the boat, the shirtless blond moved to stand at the deck's ladder. It turns out he was dressed in a skimpy bright orange Speedo. "Can you take me to shore?" he asked, in Castilian rather than in Catalan as Jaume and I had been speaking. "The water's full of jellyfish."

I looked him over, and from my angle I got a good look at certain parts. Which, I had to admit, looked quite nice from here.

Jaume and I have been together nearly two years, during which time we've tried a number of different relationship options, from complete monogamy to a period when we were hardly having sex with each other we were slutting around so much. This led to a trial separation and eventual reunion under our current agreement: whenever we want something outside our relationship, we do it together. Which doesn't mean that we always wind up in threesomes, although that is usually the case. Sometimes we might go to a sauna together, and maybe each of us pick up someone; the cabinas aren't really big enough for all four of us to go into one and have our two separate pairings, but the one time we tried it was pretty exciting watching Jaume get fucked by someone else while he watched me fuck the trick I'd picked up. I still felt some jealousy, but at the same time I felt Jaume was including me in his pleasure and vice versa.

Most of the time, we were happiest with the more traditional threesome, and our taste was similar enough that we didn't have too many disagreements—at least among ourselves. It was not always the easiest thing convincing our prospective third, but actually many guys have a fantasy about doing threesomes. They're not always so easy to come by in the typical bar or dance club scenario (as opposed to, say, a sauna, where they're easier to arrange), so many men were willing to give it a shot when we asked them. I always think they took one look at Jaume and decided they'd put up with sharing him for a chance at sex with him, half a cake being better than no cake. I'm just glad I'm a deciding voice in who I share him with.

Since both Jaume and I have active libidos, we're usually up for anything attractive the other proposes. So I boldly asked our blond boatman, "And what's our fee for the taxi service?" in Castilian while rubbing my crotch with one hand in an unmistakable gesture. Jaume, looking over his shoulder at me, glanced down into my lap and smiled, his silent agreement to what I'd proposed, then looked up at the guy on the deck as we waited for an answer. He looked down at the bulge growing in my skimpy blue swimtrunks, glanced out at the shore for a moment, then back at Jaume and me.

"OK," he nodded, "come on up," and he stepped away from the side of the boat.

I, too, looked back at the shore, my mind crowding with thoughts: I wondered what people could see from the beach. I wondered if anyone would see us board the boat and especially if the kayak crew would get mad at us for abandoning ship. I wondered if our stuff, still on the beach, was safe. I wondered about the wisdom of climbing onto a boat full of strange men; what if they were the proverbial axe-murderers, who dumped the body bits overboard where the fishes ate up the evidence? I wondered what our prospective passenger looked like without his bathing suit, and I nudged Jaume in the back with my paddle. "Let's go," I said.

We tied the kayak to the bottom rung of the ladder and then climbed up it, taking the paddles with us. The last thing we needed was for a wave to knock them into the water while we were up on the boat, leaving us *all* stranded. Besides, I figured if we had them with us, it would be more trouble for one of the guys on the boat to steal the kayak. I was still feeling a little suspicious. But I've always been cautious: Even with tricks on land, I was wary if I brought them home, making sure there were no easily-pocketed valuables lying about and guarding my wallet someplace unexpected. I'd never had any problems, but it didn't hurt to be on the safe side, I thought, even when walking on the wild side.

I followed Jaume onto the deck. We were surrounded by a group of maybe seven men—some in swimsuits, like we were, others in more ordinary summer clothes. They were all eyeing us, as if they were feeling suspicious, too. And who could blame them? Or was there something more than curiosity in their gaze? How much of our interchange had they overheard? And what did they think of it, those who'd heard and understood?

The guy who wanted a ride stood with the rest of them, but he didn't really blend into the crowd. Maybe it was because he was the only one I recognized—he had an identity separate from that of the group because I'd first seen him alone, leaning over the side of the boat as he called out to us. Also, he stood a step apart from them physically, as if to underscore the fact that he was leaving, and they would stay. As I took in the other men—who were as varied a lot of homosexual types as one could imagine, from an overdressed, highly coifed queen to a quiet butch number who looked like an ultra-straight soccer player—I wondered if he'd always been part of this mixed crew or if he'd swum out here. I glanced at his crotch, but his swimsuit was dry. All that meant was that he'd been onboard long enough to dry out. As I watched, I thought his basket gave a small jump, as if in anticipation of what we planned, and I smiled, as much at the thought of our imminent sex as the idea of how I imagined this was making him feel. I glanced at the other men as I idly rubbed my crotch, but got no sexual connection from any of them. Suddenly, I wondered less why he wanted to go ashore.

Our blond made no move to introduce us or himself, and I wondered if we were planning to do whatever it was we would do there in front of everyone. It would hardly be the first time we had an audience, so it didn't really faze me, and I was sure it wouldn't be much of a problem for Jaume either. I reached over and helped him unbuckle the life jacket, letting it fall to the deck. It made a small clatter as the buckles hit the wood, and the noise seemed startling in the absence of any social chatter. Jaume hadn't moved and was still straddling the strap that had gone between his legs, which now made two separate circles connecting to the life jacket. As I looked at Jaume's muscular thighs I imagined him as the famed Colossos of Rhodes straddling the strait. What a sight it must have been to sail between those massive thighs and gaze upwards!

I reached down and fondled Jaume's cock through the fabric of his green swimsuit, staring defiantly at the men around us. Like me, Jaume was half-hard already and I could feel his dick respond to my fingers. The men said nothing—content, it seemed, to be voyeurs and nothing more. Even the blond in the orange bathing suit was silent, although he watched my hand as it moved, looking up every now and then to meet my stare and then letting his gaze drop once more. Finally, he moved closer to us and dropped to his knees before Jaume. I pulled the green nylon down over Jaume's hips and his cock sprang free of the confining fabric. The blond reached out to hold it, and I looked up at the crowd around us, expecting them to respond in some way, but they were all as still as statues. It would've been much more normal for them to try and be involved, or to comment in some way, to somehow indicate that they were, if not exactly participating, at least present and aware. Even pointedly ignoring us, carrying on their conversation as if we were not fornicating in their midst, would be a more direct acknowledgment.

I put them out of mind and looked down at Jaume's ass clenching and unclenching as he thrust his cock into the blond's mouth. My cock grew longer at the sight of my lover's cock being worshiped by this stranger's mouth, and it poked out from the side of my swimsuit. I still had my life jacket on, so I couldn't actually pull the trunks down the way I'd done with Jaume, since the strap that ran between my legs prevented this. But I pulled my cock and balls free through one of the leg holes and started pulling at my dick; I didn't want to bother with the hassle of untangling the jacket, and the tight fabric of the swimsuit's leg hole against the base of my cock was a pleasurable pressure.

The blond still wore his orange swimtrunks as he sucked off my boyfriend. As if my glancing at his cock awakened some sixth sense in him, he seemed to realize that my cock was also loose and seeking attention, and without either looking up or breaking his rhythmic motions along Jaume's cock, he reached out and grabbed hold of mine with unerring precision, as if he'd all this time been completely aware of where it was in relation to him. This was a skill I often admired in men who had it, like the ability to locate another man's nipples through his shirt without groping around.

I looked up again at the men around us as the blond jerked on my dick, but it was as if time had stopped as far as they were concerned, for all the life they showed. I glanced at their crotches to see if at least we were providing them with a good spectacle, but it was hard to tell if they were aroused or not. As if he could tell that my attention had wandered away, the blond's tugging at my dick changed, and suddenly he pulled me forward by my cock until I had to shift my stance; I stumbled forward and suddenly I was sliding into the wet of his mouth. I watched his lips work their way up and down my shaft, and looking past his face I could see the outline of his own dick, obviously hard, within his orange swimsuit. But he made no move to take it out or even touch himself through the fabric. I was glad, judging from his arousal, that he was obviously enjoying some aspect of this scene. And then I closed my eyes and stopped worrying and let myself enjoy the slippery magic of his tongue on my cock. With my eyes still closed I reached out and found Jaume's pierced tit, as if I'd suddenly acquired that skill that had always amazed me, although I think it was simply because the piercing made for a much larger area for my fingers to find. I tugged at the silver loop gently and smiled and opened my eyes and found my lover smiling back. I grabbed him by the neck and pulled him toward me for a kiss.

Below us, the blond had grabbed both of our dicks and was jerking us off as he caught his breath. Or perhaps he was simply considering, weighing our cocks in his fists as he contemplated his next move. He tugged our cocks until we were standing close to one another, then put both of us in his mouth at once. It's a strange feeling, because it's not as wonderful as having a pair of lips clamped tightly around the shaft of your cock, but sharing something so intimate with my lover made the experience even more intense. Jaume's and my own tongues locked as the blond ran his back and forth over the sensitive crowns, pulled free from their foreskin by the state of our arousal. I could feel my breath quicken in those moments leading up to orgasm, and I grabbed my own dick with one hand and began to jerk myself off. Jaume followed suit, and I looked down at the blond to see how he was responding, thinking that he might be touching himself, but he seemed to be just watching us jerk off and enjoying the sight from his crotch-level view. But then he leaned forward and began to suck on my balls, and after a few more moments I was sending short white arcs of cum onto the wooden deck. I made a sort of grunt into Jaume's throat with each spasm that went through my cock, and even with my eyes closed in ecstasy I could tell that Jaume had quickened the pace of his hand's motion. Soon his tongue was pressing deeply into my mouth as he, too, came.

The blond was still kneeling before us, smiling widely. And suddenly, now that the sex was over, the other passengers suddenly came to life. I didn't quite understand the noise at first, lost in the afterglow of orgasm, but I soon made out words and realized they were talking to each other again, going about things as usual, although still keeping an eye turned toward us every now and then. Maybe it was because Jaume's and my cocks were still bare for all to see, mine already shrinking now that I'd cum but Jaume's still a rigid pole; he always took a while for it to go down. "Well, that was certainly worth a first-class trip to the shore," I announced. The blond smiled again and climbed to his feet. I wondered for a moment if he were planning to kiss us, and half-hoped he would, since it would make the encounter feel suddenly more . . . personable. But the moment passed and he turned toward the others.

Jaume bent forward and pulled his swimsuit up. He stepped into the loops of the life jacket and I helped him into it, as the blond said goodbye to his friends. I watched him kiss them farewell, some on either cheek and some directly on the lips, and wondered what each man must feel, knowing where his mouth had been just moments before. Were they disgusted? Jealous? Indifferent, as they'd been while watching us? I wasn't sure. And it didn't really matter.

Jaume and I descended first to resume our places with the paddles. I wondered for a moment what would happen if we simply took off before the blond descended. It was not as if there were anything truly binding us to wait for him, other than our word. What could he do, complain to the police that he had given us each blow jobs and we wouldn't take him to shore in return? It wasn't as if he'd dive in after us, since he was afraid of the jellyfish. And with reason, I noticed, watching a ghostly white shadow bloom in the water next to our kayak.

We waited for him, an honorable exchange as we'd agreed, and once he'd settled himself on the little ridge between the seats we began paddling and pulled away from the boat. His friends called out after him, and there were other shouts and noises and sounds of frivolity from the men we couldn't see from our lower vantage. Suddenly the boat seemed like a lively and fun place, quite the opposite of how it had been when we were aboard. Had we been the inhibiting force? Maybe it was our passenger. It didn't really matter. My lover and I had enjoyed our private encounter there amidst the crowd, and I at least had no regrets.

Our strokes had pulled us nearly to the shore. "Thanks," our passenger said as he leaped off the kayak into the shallow water and waded the last few feet onto the sandy beach. He turned around and waved at us, and back at the pleasure boat, and then walked up the sand. I wondered briefly what plans he had here, if maybe we'd see him again later at the dance. Or any of those men from the boat....

One of the kayak crewmen came jogging over and yelled at us for coming this close to the beach. He told us we had to head out to deeper waters or bring the kayak back to the launch. We pushed off, Jaume and I, paddling back out among the higher waves and the ghostly jellyfish. The sky was crystal blue, the sea was warm, my boyfriend was with me, and we'd just had a threesome with a sexy blond. On the beach behind us was a party celebrating being gay: it was one of those perfect moments.

We weren't paddling in any direction, just sort of enjoying being out on the surf. After a while, Jaume looked over his shoulder at me and asked in Catalan, "Think we should go back to the boat and see if anyone else needs a lift?"

I smiled at Jaume, and without a word I stuck my paddle into the water like a rudder again, turning our course back toward that boat at my lover's request.

When the Cat's Away . . .

My boyfriend was in Los Angeles for two weeks on business, and by Wednesday of the first week I was desperately lonely and missing him. And I was horny as hell.

We lived together, and while we didn't have sex every night, we did have intimacy every day, the low-key domestic intimacy of holding each other as we watched the news, of brushing against one another in the bed we shared, even the simple fact of having each other in the same space. Now that he was gone, I realized how much I missed picking up after him, since it meant that he was here or had been here, even if I didn't see him at that very moment. In the few days that Kevin had been in Los Angeles, I had long ago cleaned up any casual indicators of his presence. Sure, all his stuff was still here, but it was all too neatly in place—where *I* had placed it, since Kevin was so cavalier about his living environs. I missed the small messes he made to show his presence, like leaving a string of dental floss floating in the toilet, waiting to be flushed away.

I didn't just miss his presence and constant companionship. I missed his body. I missed waking up next to him and feeling his early-morning piss boner pressing against my thigh. I missed waking up before him and lifting aside the sheets, licking my way down his flat abs to that boner, aching for release, and sucking him awake. And some mornings, after drinking his cum, I kept his dick in my mouth as it went soft, wouldn't let go until he'd unloaded his night's bladder down my throat, washing away the sweetness of his cum with the brine of his piss.

His body was always so present. He liked to strip to his t-shirt when he came home from work, leaving his suit, shirt, and tie rumpled on the couch or floor, wherever they had fallen. He even stripped off his underwear, childish BVD briefs he still wore, out of habit, though he was certainly no longer a boy. His thick, floppy cock attested to that, and all evening long I'd get glimpses of it, dangling low and peeking out from beneath the edge of his thin t-shirt, worn almost sheer with age. I couldn't get enough of him, of watching him, of feeling him, even after living with him for four years.

We'd settled, as it seems all domestic couples eventually do, into not having sex all the time, letting the tension and pressure and desire for each other build to make the sex more intense. Watching him lounge about the apartment, though, careless in his nudity, always brought an ache to my balls. Kevin lacked self-consciousness about his body, which is one of the qualities I found most appealing about him. Of course, he had a finely shaped body, smooth and lean, developed by years as a runner in high school and refined by regular workouts at the gym. But there were plenty of guys I knew with seemingly-perfect bodies who didn't have his ease, his naturalness with himself and his sexuality. I certainly had nowhere near that level of comfort, although I was perfectly at ease being naked with him, and tried to be in that state with him whenever possible. So, sex might happen at any time of day or night, in any room of the house.

Now I spent every night alone on the couch, wanting to feel him lying next to me. Though I stared at the television set, I didn't see the news. Instead, my mind replayed images of sex we'd had together.

As he stood at the stove one night, sautéing onions and other vegetables for a sauce, I came up behind him and cupped the cheeks of his ass, ran my fingers over the layer of short coarse hairs that covered them. Squatting down behind him, I pressed my face into the crack, inhaling the scent of the light sweat that covered him from the heat of the stove. My tongue darted forward as I used my hands to pry the mounds apart. I licked up and down, my tongue flickering across the sensitive bud of his asshole and moving on, wetting down the entire region thoroughly before narrowing in on my target. His cheeks clenched involuntarily as I struck home, and he thrust his hips forward, pushing himself toward the stove.

"Careful of the fire," I murmured into his ass, though I don't know if he heard me.

My tongue darted back to his hole, working deeper and deeper inside as his muscles relaxed into the pleasure. "Mmm," he groaned, pressing his entire body back against my tongue as if he were trying to impale himself on it.

When I'd worked him for a while, I stood up and reached around him for the jug of olive oil. I poured some on my cock, which had been eagerly at the ready ever since I first saw his naked buns calling to me as he cooked. I pressed my slicked cock against his ass, rubbing it back and forth along the crack and over his asshole, spreading the oil. Kevin lowered the flame under the vegetables and continued to stir them as he leaned forward, lifting his ass for me. I took aim and slid my cock slowly inside him, pushing until it disappeared from view. We stood frozen like that for a long moment, and Kevin squeezed with the muscles of his ass. He let go of me, and I began to pull out, slowly still, so that he was aware of my cock's every inch and movement, aware of the void it left behind and aching for me to fill him up again.

Which, of course, I did. Soon, Kevin was gripping the edge of the stove with both hands to balance himself as I pumped in and out, fast and hard. Sometimes I'd pull nearly out and jab with just the swollen glans of my dick, letting his sphincter thrill the thick sensitive crown. And then I'd thrust inside of him again, filling him as deeply as he could take me until we were the same being, my chest pressed against his back, our bodies slick with the sweat from our fucking and the heat of the stove. My cock was planted far inside of him, and I was content to leave it there, no thrusting or friction, just the firm squeezing of his ass against the base of my cock. I grabbed his cock in one hand, squeezing it tight, and tickled his balls with my other. We ground our hips together, a slow gentle twist that sent a totally different thrill through my cock than the swift thrusts.

I felt Kevin's balls tighten, and I increased my grip on his cock, massaging its length. My other hand I flicked across the underside of his balls, which had pulled up until they were nestled on either side of his cock. I stood on my tiptoes, shifting the position of my dick inside him, as if I were going to lift him off his feet on my cock. That pushed him over the edge, and he began to shoot. The first spurt arced onto the stove, where it sizzled. I pulled at his cock, pointing other spurts onto the oven door and floor, away from the dangerous flames. But something about hearing the sizzling cum, or the smell of his semen mixing with the aromas of dinner, or the pulses his ass sent through my cock as he orgasmed, sent me over the edge, too, and my balls unloaded themselves inside of Kevin, long, exhausting, exhilarating pulls of semen shooting from my body into his.

"That was really hot," Kevin said, twisting around to kiss me, my cock still inside of him. Then he pulled off me, turned fully around and kissed me again, and told me to order take-out. Dinner had burned while we fucked. Hot, indeed!

How I wanted Kevin here now! How my cock wanted Kevin here now!

I switched off the television. I'd been stroking myself, idly, through my sweatpants. Without Kevin and his easy nakedness, I'd reverted to wearing loose clothing when lounging about the house.

I stood up, my cock tenting my sweatpants. It had no doubts about what I should do now, with or without Kevin. But I was tired of jerking off. I'd done that two or three times each day the weekend that Kevin left. Now I wanted the connection with another body that sex provided.

When Kevin and I moved in together, solidifying our relationship, we established certain ground rules. Sex outside the relationship was permissible—with caveats. We must always practice safer sex, and this included no sucking someone else off without a condom, even though unprotected oral sex is thought to be very low-risk. We had each tested negative for HIV before we moved in together, and again half a year later, and these ground rules were our way of establishing and maintaining the trust that allowed us to have unprotected sex with each other.

If we had sex outside the relationship, we had to tell each other, immediately, especially if we slipped up and did something unsafe. That had been a touchy subject, but necessary.

One time I just couldn't help myself: I was fooling around with this guy who suddenly slipped his dick up my ass, and I was enjoying it so much I didn't make him stop. I didn't let him cum inside me, of course, but it was still a definite risk, especially since the guy's cock had leaked so much precum.

I'd been torn about whether to tell Kevin, but I realized I had to. It wouldn't be fair, especially if I had actually caught something which I might pass on to him. We had a huge fight, which was good for us, because it let us show our commitment for each other. If we hadn't meant for it to be OK to have sex outside the relationship, we shouldn't have made it possible, but we both enjoyed the occasional trick—it revitalized our own sex life. We were fighting not because of what I'd done, but because of what it meant for our own sex for the next few months. We would have a fear of fluids for the next half year. No more languid sixty-nining. No more heat-of-the-passion fucking, either; now everything had to be planned: we had to have condoms handy, and water-based lubes.

And for the next six months, Kevin and I practiced safe sex. I was still able to suck him off and even swallow his cum, because Kevin had been well-behaved. But since we didn't know my serostatus, everything related to me was latex-wrapped. When I tested negative again six months later, we decided it was safe enough to go back to fucking without condoms again. I don't know what I enjoyed more that night, the feel of Kevin's tongue on my cock, slick with saliva, or the feel of my cock up his ass without a condom. They were both heaven. And I was determined not to lose those pleasures again.

I'd never been much into anonymous, as opposed to casual, sex. I'd flirted with it before, of course—how could you not, visiting any bar with a backroom. The curiosity to check it out was too strong to resist—but I had never felt much need for it. I never had a problem finding tricks to pick up, but that required so much more investment than what I wanted right now. I wasn't looking for a fling. I just wanted to feel a body next to mine, to hold a cock in my hands. I'd love to feel a cock in my mouth, but I wouldn't, not tonight, and I knew that.

I untied the string on my sweatpants and let them go. They started to fall but got caught on my erection, which held them up in front, leaving my ass bare. I laughed and undid the fabric, stepping out of them completely. My balls were already pulled tight against my body, aching for release. I pulled on jeans, not bothering with underwear, and tucked my erect cock down the left pants leg. I buttoned the jeans and then stroked the bulge through the denim. I was so aching for action, I wondered if my cock wouldn't stay hard with anticipation even during the long subway ride to the bars.

I pulled on a white t-shirt and my leather jacket, which I planned to check as soon as I got where I was going. Kevin and I aren't bar hoppers, since neither of us is a heavy drinker— wine with dinner, of course, and socially, but not just for the sake of getting plastered, and hardly ever beer. But we have friends who are still single, intentionally or otherwise, and they keep us up to date as to what bars are happening and which are duds, and of course there are the local rags. One bar in particular was touted for its downstairs backroom, an entire floor devoted to the pleasures of anonymous flesh.

The subway seemed jam-packed with good-looking men. Of course, it was just that I was horny, so I was focusing on what it was about every man I saw that made him attractive. It might be something as simple as the bulge in his crotch or something as ineffable as the way he held his hands in his lap that made me want to feel those hands dancing across my skin. I flirted with some of the guys, just to pass the time, but wasn't seriously cruising any of them. I wasn't interested in that right now, actually, much as I was desperate to get laid. I didn't want to go through the effort of picking someone up, of dealing with someone as a person. I wanted just a warm and willing body.

At the bar, however, I cruised in earnest, looking for someone to bring down into the lower level and undress. But my pursuit came up fruitless. There's something different about cruising on the subway or the streets, places whose express purpose isn't built around sexual attraction. In those locales, cruising is exhilarating. Even if I'm rejected haughtily, or being cruised by someone who doesn't interest me, there's that moment of recognition of sexual interest that I find so comforting. In some ways, it's like gaydar, but there's something a little more active in cruising—an outpouring of affability, of sexualizing energy and appreciation. In a bar, however, cruising is a more desperate affair. There's a single-mindedness that I find offputting. Besides, I wasn't finding anyone I wanted to pick up.

I wandered to the lower level. At the bottom of the stairs was a short hallway, with bathrooms to the left and a door to the right. A black sheet was hung across the doorway, and I pushed it aside and walked through. The area beyond was a dimly lit room whose walls had been painted black. I paused near the threshold, waiting for my eyes to adjust to the almost-light. Someone brushed past me from behind, coming into the room as I had just done and unable to see me, as his eyes hadn't adjusted yet. However, as his body came into contact with mine, he reacted instinctively and reached out to touch me, to feel my back, the muscles of my arm, groping. His hand dropped down to touch my ass.

I walked away, ignoring him. He didn't follow. I stepped toward a wall, and again a hand reached out and touched me. I looked into the darkness and realized there were people lined against the wall, dark shapes against a darker background. I shied away from this new hand as well, looking for a bare space to lean against. Twice I accidentally brushed against another body, which turned toward me like a flower turning toward the sun, eager to engage me in sex. Each time I pulled back, not yet ready.

I'm not sure what was holding me back. Perhaps it was seeing the crowd upstairs, and knowing that this group must be made up of men pretty much like them. I'm not a body-fascist—in that there are many different types of men I'm attracted to, and many things about men that I find attractive—but overall I'm pretty visual, I think, and I like to see a man I'm having sex with. The idea of putting a cock in my mouth that I can't admire first, can't hold in my hand and appreciate, just doesn't appeal to me. Which was fine right now, since I wasn't going to be putting any cocks in my mouth. But I wanted to feel one in my hand, wanted to feel another man's hand on my own cock, pressing against my asshole or up inside it, twisting my nipples.

As my eyes grew accustomed to the dimness, I began to see the men around me. Like me, they mostly stuck to the edges like a bunch of wallflowers. In one or two cases, backs faced me. I realized I was staring at two men who were engaged in some sort of sex. I watched the thrusting of hips towards the wall, wondering what the guy against the wall must feel like, wondering what it would feel like to have someone stand in front of me and rub his crotch against mine, on display to everyone. I think that's part of why I wasn't yet hard, really—the idea of other people watching to get off on my having sex. I've been part of orgies before, but in those situations everyone's taking part, and you can see all that's happening. You're meant to, there's an exhibitionism to it all. There was a different feeling about this sex around me, though, as if so many of these men were here not just to have sex, although that's what we all were hoping for, but to be in the presence of sex. And I was one of them. I had this desperate yearning to be part of the sex, but right then all I could do was be in the presence of sex, which had its own sort of fascination.

I watched the men cruising the wallflowers, some walking around with their dicks out, stroking themselves. I could see the motion of arms pumping among the wallflowers as well, men jerking off from being in the presence of sex, keeping themselves hard and ready in case an interested hand or mouth came near, or perhaps attempting to attract someone with the motion. Any sex drew attention. Watching one of the cruising men suddenly connect with a wallflower near me, everyone in the vicinity shifted. We were all aware of the sudden union, and focused on their coitus. Men moved in to reach out towards the pair, to touch an ass or chest, as if hoping their sexual success might rub off on them, like patting the belly of Buddha for luck. Sometimes it was to encourage the pair in their endeavors, or to encourage the pair to reach out and embrace an additional partner.

I, too, was drawn to the sex nearby. I looked for silhouettes, for the outline of a cock being jerked in someone's hand. As I was watching one cluster of men, having stepped away from my place along the wall to get a better view, a hand reached from behind to grab my crotch. My back stiffened, but I stopped myself from pulling away. I didn't encourage the guy, exactly, but I didn't stop him. His hand drifted up and down my crotch, trying to work my cock to stiffness. I don't know if it was his hand that did it or watching the silhouettes of the cocks before me, the cluster of bodies, of men who'd abandoned themselves to sex. I started to get hard. I stopped being someone who was here to be in the presence of sex, and became someone who was here to have sex. It didn't matter who I was having sex with, it was having sex that mattered. So people were watching; it's not as if they could see much anyway. And what the fuck if they

could? That's what we were all here for, that's what we were all
here doing. I felt suddenly liberated and thought I understood
some degree of Kevin's ease with his nudity.

Thinking about Kevin suddenly brought my cock to life,
and the guy unzipped my pants and drew my swollen dick out
into the air. I felt as if the attention of the room focused on it
for a moment, and I relished that attention and admiration. I
let my own hands reach out and feel the crotch of the guy groping me. His cock was already out of his pants, kept at attention
by a leather cockring that thrust his balls forward. His cock was
thin, the size of two fingers, more or less, but enough length
to stroke. It didn't matter. I wasn't looking for perfection, I was
looking for contact, pure and simple. He was uncut, and I spent
some time playing with his foreskin, rubbing it back and forth
over the crown of his dick, letting the precum spill over onto my
hand. I ran my slicked fingers down the length of his cock until
they bounced against his balls. I dropped his shaft to tickle his
balls, wetting them down with the almost-dry precum.

I felt a hand on my own balls then, and realized that the
guy had not let go of my cock. Someone else had joined us,
and I reached out to feel who it was. I connected with a bare
chest, a t-shirt whose front had been pulled over the guy's head,
and I began to stroke his bare pecs. My fingers grazed against
stubble, a triangle of hair he shaved to show off his muscles. A
ring of stubble surrounded his nipples, and the left one had
a ring in it. I twisted the tit with the ring between the fingers of
one hand, and squeezed the other guy's cock in my other hand.
Both of them were playing with my own cock and balls, and a
hand was rubbing across my ass. I wondered where the first
guy's other hand was, but it didn't matter. He was probably
stroking the other guy. Which is what he should be doing, I
thought.

Still pulling on the first cock with one hand, I let my hands drift down the chest of the other guy to his crotch. I wanted a cock in each hand as I was getting jerked off. I sprung the button on the guy's pants, and they fell open; he'd already unzipped the zipper. I reached into his boxers for his cock, feeling a nice hefty one through the fabric. I pulled it through the slit in the boxers, wishing for some light so I could take a look and admire it. I glanced down to see its silhouette but couldn't see anything against the dark floor. It didn't matter. I could see with my fingers, which were now gazing at a Renoir or Matisse painting, a great work of art.

I let go of the other guy's thin cock to bring both hands to play on this new one—the better to see you with, I thought—and I smiled even though no one could see me. I turned toward this second man, positioning my body against his. Pairing off. The first guy who engaged me felt slighted, I guess, but I didn't care. He got to feel my body for a while. He got to touch my cock, massive compared to his, though certainly no monster compared to some I've been fucked by in my time. We had no promises of completion. This was not a pick-up, where we've implicitly agreed, in going home with one another, to try for a mutual ejaculation.

The first guy's hands still reached for me, reached around my back for my cock, but my attention was focused on the guy before me, and he held my complete attention. Or I should say that I held his attention, quite literally, squeezing along his cock with both hands. There's something about a cock of a certain size that's a marvel just to feel and hold. It doesn't have to be gargantuan, but it needs to have a certain heft to give this feeling. And this guy's cock certainly was big enough, a delight just to hold. I would've loved to sink down to my knees and take him in my mouth, but I knew I couldn't. I didn't know anything about this guy, who he was or what his serostatus might be. I didn't even know what he looked like. But I held his cock in my hands, and he was tugging on mine, and that was a wonderful thing to be doing.

He suddenly let go of my cock, though, and put his hands on my shoulders, pressing down. He wanted me to suck him off, and I wondered how he'd sensed my desire. But I shook my head, and shrugged his hands off my shoulders. He stopped pressing down, and I pulled on the tip of his cock, my fingers thrilling the sensitive crown. After a moment he pulled his beautiful cock out of my hands and tucked it back into his pants. I felt, for an instant, as crushed and rejected as the guy I'd turned my back on just a moment before. My fingers curled around empty air, remembering feel and heft, and I was jealous of the next man this guy paired up with.

I looked around, looking for sex again. My cock was still hard, and still out of my pants. A short, heavyweight guy walked past me, and his fingers groped my crotch. They closed about my cock, and I tried to pull it out of his hands. I wasn't interested. Having held that beautiful cock in my hands, I was now looking for perfection again, not just contact with anyone. But the guy didn't let go of my cock, he sunk to his knees in front of me, and before I could pull back had wrapped his lips around my dick.

He knows nothing about me, I thought. But I knew I was safe, and my guilt didn't last long as his tongue worked its way up and down my shaft, slicking my cock down. His lips clenched tightly around my dick and worked their way down to the base before pulling back. He wasn't someone I would ordinarily have wound up having sex with, but it didn't seem to matter. Tonight I just wanted a mouth on my cock and a cock in my hands. I might want a cock in my mouth, want to sink down on my knees and take any hard cock into my mouth like this guy had done. I wanted that beautiful thick cock I'd held, wanted to suck it and feel it inside me, but I knew it wasn't to be, that I'd never do it because I wouldn't feel safe doing it, wouldn't want to take that risk. But that was fine. Right now I had a mouth on my cock, which was exactly what I wanted. I reached out and grabbed the guy's head and began to fuck his face, not merely taking a blow job off this stranger, letting him decide to suck me off, but taking the active role in this encounter.

He murmured something, but it wasn't a complaint so I didn't stop. I pounded into his face, pushing deep into his throat, hardly giving him a chance to breathe. I pulled out all the way and lifted my cock away from his face. He whimpered, as if he were a child whose favorite toy I'd just taken away. "Lick my balls," I said. My voice was not loud, but in the quiet of the room—the utter silence except for the rustle of clothing as men shifted, waiting for sex, and the sounds of fists and mouths pumping cocks—it commanded all attention. Men drifted towards us, as the guy on his knees did as I told him. I slowly stroked my cock, slick with this stranger's saliva, as he took each testicle into his mouth and then let it go. Men stood nearby, their crotches poised at the ready for the cocksucker to do them next. Hands reached around to cup my ass and squeeze my tits, and I pointed my cock down the guy's throat again. He started pumping away on my shaft, and I let him go at me like that, enjoying his worship of my dick and all these hands on my body. Letting him suck me off instead of actively fucking his face left my hands free to roam, and I sent them each in search of a cock. Again, I wanted to hold a cock in each hand while this guy sucked me off, to connect in sex with three strangers.

I undid zippers and fondled crotches, looking for those two cocks. The guy's mouth kept working, up and down along my cock. I grabbed onto a cock with my right hand, held it tight as if it were an anchor, and thrust my hips back and forth into the stranger's mouth, pushing my crotch upwards until his nose squashed against my belly. My other hand found a cock that was already out of some guy's pants and hard, waiting for some action, and I began to tug on it. I felt, for a moment, like a kid trying to pat his head with one hand while making circles on his belly with the other. And I felt childish glee at being able to do so. I was in sensory overload, and it was heaven.

The guy who was sucking my cock pulled off to catch his breath. Almost immediately, a guy who'd been standing nearby moved forward, thrusting his prick in front of the guy on his knees. I guess he hadn't really needed to catch his breath all that much, for he swallowed this new guy's prick immediately. I was disappointed that someone had stolen my cocksucker, but right then my hands were both busy, stroking and pulling on two nice cocks, and I didn't want to risk letting go of either of them, so I didn't have a free hand to take my cocksucker back.

It turns out not to have mattered, because the guy whose cock was now being sucked suddenly leaned forward and began to suck my dick. The idea of this daisy chain, of someone whose cock was being sucked sucking on my cock, really turned me on, and I felt my balls tighten. I began to tug harder and faster on the cocks in each of my hands, and I heard breaths quicken all around me. The new cocksucker was even better than the last one, or perhaps it was just that my cock was harder since I was so close to coming, but it felt great. I wanted to feel a cock in my own mouth, and I imagined sucking off Kevin, thought about having sex with him the moment he came off the plane. The image of Kevin's cock in my mouth brought me close to the edge.

"I'm gonna cum," I said, as a courtesy to the guy whose mouth was on my cock. He didn't know me from Adam, after all, and he had no way to know I'd tested negative and practiced only safe sex. The guy didn't pull off my cock, as I'd expected, but pushed even deeper onto me, thrusting my dick far into his throat. Knowing I was negative, I didn't feel much guilt. I pulled on the cocks in each of my hands and thought about sucking on Kevin's big cock. Suddenly my balls let loose and my hips bucked as I shot my cum down this stranger's throat, a stranger whose own cock was being sucked as he sucked on mine. He bobbed up and down on my cock, milking it of every drop of cum. Only when I had begun to go soft did he let it fall from his mouth and stand up. He started pumping away at the face of the guy who was sucking on his own dick. I turned my attention to the two men whose dicks I still held in my hands. Not for any desire of reciprocity, but because I wanted to feel their cum rushing over my fingers, wanted the satisfaction of having brought them to orgasm.

I'd have to bring Kevin here sometime, I thought. The idea of being on hand while some guy sucked Kevin off, to have some stranger give us a tag-team blow job, to have two guys sucking each of us off, to kiss him while each of us was being sucked off, to be here, in the presence of sex, and for me to suck him off while he held another man's cock in his hands—there were infinite possibilities, all of which seemed intensely arousing just then, and I felt my cock begin to stiffen again with renewed life.

Cruising the Clinic

I hadn't expected to be cruising the STD clinic, but then I'd never really thought much about the place before I arrived. I mean, I always practice safer sex—or so I thought—and didn't think I'd ever need to go to one of these places, although I knew they existed. But I called the hotline listed in the phone book on Monday morning because I was too embarrassed to go to my regular doctor and show him the painful red spots on my dick that had shown up just before the weekend—ruining any chance of my going out and getting laid!

Evidently, I wasn't the only fag who had the same idea, although there were plenty of straights waiting too—both men and women. I half-expected to see some guy who went to my gym and was relieved to be spared that humiliation. I imagined that each of us had spent the weekend painfully examining our dicks and ruing the days or hours until the clinic opened—not to mention losing a prime summer weekend. I wondered if any of these other waiting queers had shares out on Fire Island, and thought how angry they must be to have had to stay celibate during their expensive weekend instead of slutting around in the dunes and after tea dance.

At least, I hoped they'd all stayed celibate, since they were in here to get treated for some STD. Obviously some people didn't feel that moral obligation, which is why I was in here a week after going to the West Side Club sauna and playing with a few guys. Everyone I'd had sex with looked clean; it's not as if they had sores on their dicks the way I do now. But then, as I just read in the pamphlets in both English and Spanish that littered the waiting room, with some STDs that means nothing. Even getting sucked off by someone wasn't safe. Or might not be, depending.

I wondered which of the guys around me had just caught something over the weekend, and what unsafe things they'd done to catch whatever they had....

In a chair two rows ahead of me was a guy in a tank top and beige shorts. He was short and overbuilt and covered with curly black hair. I thought he looked like the kind who liked sex messy. The kind who, if he's fucking you and pulls out to change positions and there's shit on the condom and it gets on his sheets, just shrugs and says, "Shit happens." The kind who sweats a lot when he gets excited, and likes the smell of sweat; he likes to lick your armpit, especially if you're ticklish and it makes you squirm. The kind who uses a lot of lube, who wants you to rub your cum into the thatch of hair on his chest as you're lying together in an exhausted heap after sex.

I wondered what he had. I imagined him being the sort to rim someone without thinking twice about it.

He wasn't at all my type. I couldn't really imagine having sex with him, although he looked like the kind of guy who was always ready and willing, like a rutting goat. He certainly kept giving me the eye, as if he expected we could both step into one of the examining rooms and get it on, never mind the problems that had brought us here.

More my speed was the guy sitting to my right, a preppy-looking blond who was slender but defined—his bicep filled out the cuff of his baby-blue polo shirt sleeves to good advantage. He had one of those smiles that could stop you on the street. I couldn't see it, but I hoped he had a cute round butt. He was the kind of boy you could bring home to your parents, who would bring you a long-stemmed rose on your second date, but even though he liked to go out for romantic dinners, wasn't the type to insist on getting-to-know-you before having sex. I imagined him lying on his parents' bed at their summer house where we were for the weekend. He's naked and on his back, and I'm holding his legs apart, giving me a view of his beautiful butt and his pink asshole that I'm about to plunge my condom-sheathed dick into....

I almost laughed aloud, because it was so ridiculous—even in my fantasies, I practiced safer sex! It was so unjust that I needed to be here. I hated the fact that sex was such a crapshoot these days, that it could be so dangerous. My dick was hard in my pants because of my fantasies, which made the sores hurt worse as the scabs cracked. I wished that I'd been born a couple of generations earlier, to have lived and loved during the halcyon days of the '70s, free to be as much of a sex pig as I wanted without fear.

The young Latino doctor came in and everyone looked up. He was definitely my type—I would've gladly dropped my pants for him, I thought, and then realized that I might be doing just that soon. He called a number. Short and Fuzzy stood up and followed him away.

When I looked back, the young preppy was watching me, and I smiled. He smiled back. I wondered if I could exchange phone numbers but then imagined calling and explaining where we'd met.... It seemed doomed from the start. Although if we had both caught the same thing, that would make life easier.... But what would we tell people? I know couples who met at the bathhouse, but this involved disclosing too much information. . . .

Nonetheless, I took one of the herpes pamphlets (since I was pretty sure that's what I had) and wrote, "You're cute. Call me—in a few weeks," along with my name and phone number. When my number was called, I dropped the pamphlet in his lap and was rewarded with one of his heart-stopping smiles.

A Queer Christmas Carol

Part One: Marvin's Room

Marvin Goldstein was dead, to begin with. Of that there was no doubt.

And there was no way for Scott Murphy to forget this fact, especially at this time of year, as one year was drawing to a close and another about to begin. He remembered the last Christmas he and Marvin had shared, the party they threw with Marvin's friends in the hospital room, knowing it was to be Marvin's last. Marvin was in rare form that night, kvetching and sarcastic as only a Jewish fag can be. "Here's something for you to remember me by—literally," Marvin had said, bitter and ironic, and gave all his friends yahrzeit candles as his final "Christmas" present. Which was characteristic of Marvin's sense of humor—yahrzeit's are part of the Jewish ritual of remembering their dead. The candles burn for days and are lit each year to mark the anniversary of the death. Scott didn't know if any of Marvin's other friends ever lit their candles, but each year, although not himself a Jew, he lit the yahrzeit to remember Marvin.

He did not light them on the anniversary of Marvin's death, the day itself, in the Christian calendar. Instead, he lit the yahrzeit on Hanukkah, the Jewish celebration of lights. Marvin had always hated how commercial Christmas had become. Hanukkah was not a major holiday in the Jewish calendar, but because of the secular prominence that Christmas had, Hanukkah was elevated, in terms of marketing and packaging, to a greater priority, to have a Jewish counterpart to Christmas.

Each year, Scott placed eight yahrzeits on the windowsill, and like a menorah, each night he would light another candle until all eight burned.

Yes, Marvin was dead as a doornail now, thanks to AIDS. And Scott had not had sex since his lover's death, seven years ago.

Not that he hadn't had offers. Why, that very afternoon, Christmas Eve day, while Scott worked late at the office on a project when everyone else had already gone home to their families and celebrations, one of the assistants had again tried to pick him up. Fred had been after Scott for some months now—never overbearingly, but persistent in his pursuit.

Scott was all but oblivious. Sure, he noticed the attention, and Fred's intentions, but he had long since forgotten how to act in this situation. More importantly, he had long ago lost the desire to follow these encounters through to their intense, heated climaxes.

Scott was a man who was afraid of sex. He was afraid of his desires, which were not so frightening as desires went—sexually, he liked men instead of women, a very simple thing.

But Scott no longer had sex—not with a lover, not even with himself. He had so given up any sexual activity, he had now forgotten how to enjoy the intimacy of another body, the slide of skin on skin. He could not even arouse himself.

An erection for Scott was nothing more than a bodily quirk these days, something he awoke with each morning. It was not at all sexual, only his body's mechanism to keep him from piss-ing in his sleep. Once his cock softened to allow him to relieve his bladder, it stayed soft, all day and all night.

And Scott's asshole, which once brought him so much pleasure, now was clenched tighter than Scrooge's legendary, miserly fists.

Scott was dead to pleasure, and nothing, it seemed, could wake the dead.

Scott had been raised to believe that his desire for other men was an abomination, and he could not help but fear for his soul whenever he felt this desire. And what's more, he could not help but fear for his life, for how could he enjoy sex when he was constantly afraid of AIDS?

Scott had managed to overcome his religious upbringing and love men, physically and emotionally. He had put aside his upbringing so completely that he "married" a Jew.

And the price he paid for this love was to bury this lover.

Scott could not face loving another man again, not when he couldn't know if this man would become sick and leave him, as Marvin had. He could not face sex with another man when he couldn't know if that man would infect him, accidentally, for they knew so little for certain about this disease. That risk was just too great for him.

When Fred came into Scott's office and said, "I saw the lights on. What are you doing here on Christmas Eve?" Scott did not hear him until he began to speak.

"You startled me," Scott complained, not quite turning away from his work to look at his visitor.

"Would you like to come to my place for some dinner? I'm spending the holidays alone myself, and I know I could use the company."

Though sexual tension still lurked underneath the gesture, Fred's offer was simple and genuine enough. He would be happy simply to spend the Holidays with another warm body, even if they did not have sex.

Scott had no use for companionship of any sort.

"I have work to do, and I don't celebrate the Holidays any longer." He measured the distance between two walls on the page before him.

"Well, a Merry Christmas to you," Fred said, unwilling to give up so easily. "Here's my number in case you change your mind." He wrote on a scrap of drafting paper on Scott's desk, then exited the office, leaving Scott alone.

The security guards came through at 10 P.M. and kicked Scott out of the office, so they could close the building and go home to their families. Scott gathered up all the papers on his desk, intending to continue working on them at home. He had a drafting table set up and would be able to work uninterrupted by the phone or co-workers tomorrow.

At the apartment—a co-op he'd inherited from Marvin—Scott rifled through the mail, an assortment of bills and unsolicited catalogs and advertisements. One catalog, advertising men's underwear, caught his attention for longer than he cared to admit, and the inkling of a memory began to burn within his brain. Scott ignored it. "Waste of trees!" he declared. He gathered up the offending papers and went out into the hallway, to drop them down the chute to the incinerator.

As he opened the chute's little flap on the wall, however, Scott could swear that he saw Marvin's face staring back at him. Scott blinked, trying to clear the image from his eyes. He thrust the papers down the chute as quickly as he could and slammed the little door shut. The sound seemed to echo through the entire building.

Scott hurried back to his own apartment, throwing the deadbolt once he was safely inside. He stood panting with an uncommon fear, leaning against the door as he mused upon the image he thought he saw in the chute. Impossible, of course, for Marvin was long dead; Scott had buried him himself.

Not in a Jewish cemetery; they wouldn't accept the body.

Scott remembered quite clearly how Marvin had acted out upon learning that his serostatus was positive. "The thing I've always been afraid about with tattoos," Marvin had said, "is that most of the designs I like won't age well. Things I'd regret when I'm sixty or seventy. But that's not a problem now, is it?"

Marvin had gotten a tattoo of Winnie the Pooh on his biceps, and later a band of geometric designs around his calf, and these kept him out of the Goldstein family's cemetery.

Scott heard a sound behind him, through the heavy door to the building's hallway. It was as if a doorbell were being rung, as if every doorbell in the building were ringing at the same time. His own bell began to buzz, but Scott ignored it.

He stepped away from the door as he again heard something in the hallway behind him. His buzzer continued to sound. Scott was afraid to look through the peep-hole, as if he might accidentally let whatever was out there into the apartment if he pulled aside the metal shutter to peek through the glass lens.

It didn't matter. Scott watched as whatever was out there making such a racket passed *through* the heavy door into his apartment.

"Marvin?" Scott said, his voice a whisper. "Can it be you?"

The apparition continued forward, and Scott took a step backward for each that it advanced, until he tripped on the edge of a rug and fell onto the sofa. Marvin—or rather, the ghost of Marvin, for Scott could see right through the image of his dead lover—continued to approach.

"What do you want from me?" Scott cried.

The ghost smiled. "What have I ever wanted from you, dear?" The apparition reached down into Scott's crotch, and the hand passed through the fabric of Scott's clothes to fondle his genitals. "It's been so long since we've had sex, don't tell me you're not in the mood."

Scott leaped up from the couch and crossed to the other side of the room. He clutched his head between his hands and rubbed his eyes, not believing what he saw before him.

The ghost sighed. "Please don't tell me you have a headache. Such a tired excuse. After seven years, after I come back from the dead no less, just to see you again, don't you think I deserve better than that?"

Scott's head did not merely ache, it felt as if it were about to burst asunder with incredulity and disbelief. What was he to do?

"You doubt your senses," the ghost continued, "because you have not used them to feel anything in so long. But I am quite real, have no fear of that. I am not what you should be afraid of at all."

"What do you mean by that?" Scott demanded. He took a deep breath, calming himself, as he waited for the ghost of his dead lover to answer.

"You are more dead than I am. Just look at you. When was the last time you got laid? Better yet, when was the last time you even jerked off? You're dead as a lump of coal, for all that you're still breathing. No pleasure, no feelings. I've known tombstones with more human warmth than you give off."

"How charming. You came all this way to harangue me for my sexual habits. What's the matter, not getting enough ten feet under? Serves you right for all the times you cheated on me when we were together!" Scott tried to turn away from the ghost, but found he could not quite turn his back to the phantasm;

some part of him still feared his dead lover's upset ghost, and some part of him, too, hungered for every last vision of him, even if Scott was positive this was a hallucination.

"Still so petty, I see. Nice to see some things don't change. We wouldn't want any emotional growth, now would we?" The ghost heaved a great sigh. "I didn't come here to have a fight. I came to tell you that you are wrong. I came to warn you, so that maybe you can change your future."

"What are you talking about? What do you know about my future?"

"My time is short, so I'll cut to the chase. Dickens got a lot of things right. Only I'm a Jew, so let's forget about Christmas. Instead, let's teach you about your dick. You remember the story, I'm sure: three ghosts, starting when the clock strikes One."

Marvin's ghost stood.

"But wait," Scott began. "I—"

"You had your chance," Marvin said, meaning so much. "I've pulled some strings to get you a second one. Don't mess up. Use it or lose it." The ghost turned away from him, then turned back. "And that applies to both the second chance *and* your dick."

And with that, Marvin disappeared.

Scott crossed back to the spot where Marvin had been standing. "He was just here," he whispered, hardly believing it was true. "His *ghost* was just here," he muttered, correcting himself.

Scott was afraid to go to bed. He brewed a pot of coffee. He would stay awake and greet the ghosts with a cup of coffee for each. (They could at least smell the aroma even if ghosts couldn't drink liquids anymore.) He would show them he wasn't afraid of them (especially since he knew they were coming).

But then he changed his mind and poured the coffee down the sink. He was more afraid not to follow the rules of the story.

He brushed his teeth and flossed them, staring at himself in the mirror. He wasn't as inhuman as Marvin had said he was. Was he?

Scott pulled on his flannel pajamas and double-checked the deadbolt on the front door before climbing into bed. He left the bedside light on—just in case.

A thumping sounded from against the wall he shared with his neighbors. At first, Scott was afraid it was another ghostly presence, arrived early. But then a woman's voice cried out, a howl that hovered between pain and ecstasy, and he realized it was just the woman next door having sex with her latest boyfriend. She went through a new one each month, more or less, because she wore them out so quickly.

"I'll never get to sleep now," Scott muttered, knowing from past experience that she could go on for hours. He wondered, for the first time in a long time, exactly what they were doing on the other side of the wall. . . .

And, still musing on those images, Scott fell asleep.

Part Two: Sowing Wilde Oats

His alarm clock went off, but Scott tried to ignore it. He was in the middle of some dream—he didn't quite know what it was, just that he was certain it was something he wanted to keep dreaming, if only a little while longer. Then he could get up and go to work.

"I suggest you do something about that infernal racket," a voice to his right said.

Scott bolted awake and upright, staring about the bedroom. A man stood over his bed. Scott rubbed sleep from his eyes. The man looked like a young-ish Quentin Crisp. Only Crisp wasn't dead yet, Scott was pretty sure, so his ghost couldn't be standing in Scott's bedroom.

No, it wasn't Crisp, Scott decided as he stared more closely at the stranger. Just someone with his same outdated (not to mention outlandish) fashion sense. The face was plainer, more rounded, almost owlish.

The stranger was unfazed by Scott's mute appraisal. "The machine to your left, I believe, is what you're looking for."

Scott stared at the alarm clock on his nightstand, which increased its insistent buzzing as the timer continued to tick, then turned back to the stranger in his apartment.

The visitor rolled his eyes and demanded with exasperation, "Silence that contraption already!"

Scott jerked alert and hit the snooze bar.

"Thank you," the ghost said. He moved around to the other side of the bed. "May I?" he asked, indicating the chair.

"Sure," Scott said, wondering what he'd eaten that gave him multiple hallucinations like this. Or, as Marvin might've complained: What have I done to deserve this?

Whatever it was, he still had to deal with the here and now.

Scott stood up. He didn't like feeling so out of control of the situation, so helpless. "So," he said, sitting on the edge of the bed, directly across from the spirit. "You must be the Ghost of Christmas Past."

"Indeed, you impudent pup."

Scott waved his arms. "Pish posh, old man. Let's get on with it, shall we? What have you got to show me?"

"There was a time you showed more respect for your elders," Oscar Wilde's ghost said, sternly. Scott could not help staring into the ghost's eyes, feeling himself lost in them. "Or have you forgotten?"

The room about him faded black. He could see nothing but the old man's face, his eyes, his dark hair spreading outward and seeming to envelop him in a cocoon.

Scott blinked, and when he opened his eyes he was standing in the Mineshaft. The ghost stood beside him, looking completely out of place, with his foppish scarves and billowing sleeves, amid the machismo clones and leather Daddies who prowled the bar's darkened rooms.

The phantasm nodded toward one corner, and Scott turned to follow the ghost's gaze. With a start, he saw a younger version of himself, not even twenty yet, down on his knees before a trio of older men. His hands were cuffed behind his back. Each of the men wore chaps, with nothing on underneath; their heavy balls and cocks dangled before his young face. A harness crossed the wide chest of one of the men; the other two wore leather vests. The young Scott was sucking off one of the men, hungrily wolfing down his swollen cock, while the others stroked themselves and watched, awaiting their turn. The young Scott let the cock drop from his mouth to catch his breath, but one of the other two grabbed him by his hair and pulled his head toward their crotch, guiding a dick into Scott's warm mouth.

Scott watched, amazed at his younger self's eagerness, his willingness to service these men, to do their bidding. He had hungered for their attention, for the way they forced themselves on him. He begged for it, and these men, these Daddies, made him beg, made him voice each plea.

Scott felt someone cop a feel through the flannel of his pajamas, and he glanced away from the escapades of this younger version of himself. An elaborate lace ruffle brushed against his leg as the hand was withdrawn from his crotch. Scott looked up at the ghost to express umbrage at the liberties that had been taken, when he realized that he had an erection. He'd gotten hard from watching his younger self blow that trio of older men.

"Pity an old man?" the ghost asked Scott, mockingly, while fumbling with the fastening of its trousers.

Scott opened his mouth to protest, but no sound came forth. He looked back to the corner where his younger self groveled before three men in their late forties and early fifties—men who, at the time, had seemed impossibly old to Scott.

"Yes," the ghost said, as Scott watched one of the men prepare to fuck his younger self up the ass while another continued to thrust into his mouth, "we remember now the respect that is due to our elders. Look at me when I talk to you, Boy."

Almost against his will, Scott's head swiveled—drawn by the ghost's power, and also by the authority in that command, by the memory of days when he desperately craved being in the hands of someone who would tell him what to do, someone he felt he could trust, who would protect and nurture him. Scott stared into that ghostly face, a face he could almost see through, as if it were a smoky pane of glass—a face whose eyes were a window onto another world, the world of Scott's past and the things he had done in his wilder youth.

"No," Scott said, turning away from the ghost's eyes.

The scene around them had changed. They were in his first Manhattan apartment, years before he met Marvin, which he shared with three other young gay men, all of them newly moved to the Big Apple from the Midwest. Kevin was from Ohio, and Jordan and Edward were both from Kansas.

"You cannot escape from the pleasures of the past," the ghost reminded him.

Scott could not forget.

He knew what scene would unfold before them now. That first Christmas in the apartment together, the four of them threw a wild and raucous party for all the friends, tricks, and lovers they'd made since moving to that urban gay mecca.

Scott watched, unable to turn away, as old friends got drunk and slowly began shucking their clothes. He couldn't help wondering how many of these men were still alive. He hadn't thought about them in so long.

Soon they were all naked, nearly twenty men in their twenties, having sex in a wild, messy heap.

Scott watched as this younger Scott threw himself with abandon into the fray, losing himself in the madding crowds, the press and crush of bodies and cocks, of willing mouths and asses. His younger self was intoxicated with pleasure, thrusting his cock into any nearby hand or orifice. He watched the young Scott cum, time and again, in some youth's mouth or ass. And even when his cock was too tired to rise again, the young Scott continued to play with the men around him, greedily sucking on their limp cocks, trying to coax life back into them.

"Yes, those were the days, the glory days of yore," Scott said, turning to look at the ghost who stood beside him. "The gloryhole days of yore," he quipped. "But they're gone now."

"Yes," the ghost whispered, as the world faded black around Scott once more. "They're gone now. But you cannot pretend that they never were."

"I don't—" Scott began, but he silenced himself as he knew his protestations were untrue. He turned away from the ghost's black eyes, but the world stayed dark. "Ghost, where are we now?" Scott cried out.

As his eyes adjusted to the dimness, Scott knew where they were, as he had known the apartment they just revisited, and he felt a dread foreboding in the pit of his stomach. They were in the showers of the Chelsea Gym, years later. In many ways, it was not so very different from the bathhouses he used to visit: a roomful of naked men, saunas, showers, sex. But the situation was different.

Scott knew what scene was to unfold before him. This was the trendy, fashionable gym where Scott worked out three times each week, back when he still cared enough about his body to put effort into it. When he cared about his body but had grown afraid to use it.

For months, as he worked out, he had lusted after one dark-skinned Latino man, with broad shoulders that tapered to a slim waist, a classical V-shaped torso. Scott didn't know the man's name, but he knew that body so well, had memorized every curve and shadow of it. In his mind, he had taken his pleasure from that body—for in those days Scott still took pleasure from his body. But only alone, always alone. He was afraid of other men, though he wanted them, desperately craved them.

On this day which unfolded again before Scott's eyes— though he tried to no avail to block out the visions, to lose himself in the steam and mist—this man whom he had lusted after for so very long, who quite literally had become the man of his dreams, sat next to him in the steam room.

The vision-Scott's dick began to fill with blood at the mere proximity of his idol.

And his idol took notice. The man reached down and held the vision-Scott's thickening cock in his dark hand.

Scott's own cock stood at attention as he watched, again, the beginnings of this scene he had imagined so many times. Scott had jerked off to this scenario for months, hoping and praying, but never quite believing that this day might be real.

And when it actually did happen, Scott was afraid. His mind rushed forward to those images of sex with this man that he had fantasized so many times before. But the real thing, the man himself, his body touching Scott's, was too terrifying for him. The pressure of the man's fist around his cock felt wonderful, but that feeling was not enough to combat the overwhelming fear that made Scott's dick go soft. Scott gently lifted the man's hand off his dick, smiling ruefully.

The Latin man shrugged and turned to the man sitting on the other side of him, who'd grown hard watching the two of them play. Scott watched, aghast, as the man of his dreams slipped through his grasp, hating himself for letting this opportunity disappear. He could not stop watching as these two men groped each other, fondling crotches, tweaking nipples, nibbling the flesh of each others' arms and necks.

They did nothing "unsafe." Scott could as easily have been doing these same "safe" things with this man.

But he was afraid.

Afraid of sex. Afraid of intimacy. Afraid of pleasure.

The price of fear was regret, eternal and everlasting. He would always remember having had this opportunity, and having botched it out of fear.

Regret, his sole companion of his advancing age.

"No," Scott cried out. "No. NO!"

He awoke, in his bed, as he bolted upright. His cock spasmed again. Cum squirted against the inside of his pajamas, which were tented out in front of him from his erection. His pubic hair was matted down with ejaculate.

"No," Scott whispered still. He did not want to face his fears. It was easier for him to ignore sex.

But he stared down into his lap. Could he ignore sex again, after what he'd been shown? Could he ignore sex again, now that he remembered?

His groin was suffused with the pleasurable afterglow of release.

But he was also sticky with his own cum and sweat, all that messiness of sex.

He stood up and went into the bathroom. He cleaned himself off, pulled on a dry pair of pajama bottoms, and climbed back into bed.

Part Three: (Saint) Nick

Scott awoke with the knowledge that he had just finished a dream, though he did not remember what it was. He lay in bed, eyes still closed, and thought about the events of that evening. Without opening his eyes, he reached out and pressed the snooze button, for he knew that even though the alarm was not set, the clock would buzz at 2 A.M. and rouse him. Scott had always been good at waking a few minutes before the alarm went off, to spare himself its shrill tones.

He listened to the darkness of the room about him as he lay in bed, wondering who the next ghost would be, and when it would appear. Scott realized that he could hear something, a sort of fizzing sound, like an Alka Seltzer in water. He wondered if it was the ghost already.

"Might as well get up and find out," Scott muttered.

He rolled onto his back and threw the covers off. He had a piss-erection, he noticed, though he'd taken a leak just before getting into bed an hour ago, when he awoke after the *last* ghost's visit.

He didn't feel like he had to take a piss again. But he did reach down and touch his hard cock, marveling at how good it felt simply to hold his erection in his hand, and trying not to think about how long it had been since he'd last done so.

A bead of precum stained his pajamas, where his cockhead pressed up against the fabric. The rough cotton felt so good sliding against the sensitive glans.

"I see we've taken a head start on things," a voice said from the foot of the bed. "Or should I say a hand start." The voice laughed.

Scott looked up and saw that the television was on. There was no station, just static—the crackling, fizzing sound that had woken him—and an image of a naked man, who was talking to him.

While Scott had become insensitive and impervious to sex and sexual pleasure over the last seven years, he was not completely unaware of the sex going on around him. So he recognized the naked man on his television screen as the first truly famous porn star bottom: Joey Stefano.

"Bring that over here, Big Boy, and I'll give you a helping hand myself."

It was a corny line, Scott knew, but not many men were propositioned like that by an internationally popular porn star. He was someone Scott had actually jerked off to, back in the days when he was still masturbating, if not having sex with other men.

There was something intoxicating about being approached sexually by this man so many had desired. But at the same time, he wondered if a ghost could infect a person with HIV.

What the hell, Scott thought, as he stood up and walked to the television set. He unbuttoned his fly as he walked, and pushed his erect cock so that it poked between the folds of fabric.

"That's my Boy," Joey Stefano said, reaching out from the television set to grab hold of Scott's cock. He squeezed the shaft, sending shivers down Scott's spine, and then tugged Scott by his dick into the television set.

They were now both the same size, in a small hallway.

"Pleased to meet you," Stefano said, shaking Scott's dick, which he still held. "You can call me Nick. All of my friends do." Scott remembered hearing about Joey's real name after his suicide. Nick Iaconna, that was it. There was a whole book about him now; he'd seen it in the window of a porn store he

passed on his way home from work—though, of course, he
had not stopped to examine it.

"I can't believe I'm talking to you." Scott looked down at
his dick, still being squeezed in Nick's palm. It felt like it be-
longed to someone else for all the connection he felt to it. "I
can't believe I'm doing *this* with you. I have friends who would
die to be in my place right now." He thought how he could
make a fortune from people he knew who'd pay exorbitant
sums for the chance to be where he was now.

"Actually, most of your friends are having enough fun on
their own. Look for yourself." He pointed behind Scott.

They were staring out of a television screen at Scott's co-
worker, Tim. The glass was like a window through which they
could look out at Tim's bedroom.

"He can't see us," Nick said.

"I can't believe this—you're a ghostly Peeping Tom! We
both are."

"We're peeping Tim, in this case," Nick corrected. "Peeping at Tim's pee-pee."

Scott couldn't help glancing out at the organ in question.
Tim was masturbating, completely naked on his bed as he
pulled his pud with one hand, the other massaging his ass.

"I think this is more information about Tim than I wanted
to know."

Tim had a small dick. Much smaller than average. Which
was surprising to Scott, who had assumed that Tim's prick
matched the rest of his large, over-muscled body. He began to
wonder if Tim had used steroids, which were said to make one's
genitals smaller.

"Why are we watching him?" Scott asked. Not that he could
stop himself; he was mesmerized by his co-worker's actions,
comparing them to how he would jerk off. He grabbed his own

dick, as if for reassurance. "If I'm supposed to get off from these visions, wouldn't it be better to show me some well-hung stud?"

"Anyone can find pleasure in their bodies," Nick said. "Besides, it's in the script."

"The script?" Scott asked. He looked at the ghost and suddenly realized he was talking with the Ghost of Christmas Present, and all the rest of the story. "Oh, I get it now." He struck his forehead with one palm. "I can't believe I walked into that. Tiny Tim."

Scott stared out of the television set at his co-worker. Then he turned and looked over his shoulder, and saw they were in a porn set. "Hey, you're in here twice," he said, tapping Nick on the shoulder.

Behind them, Joey Stefano was lying on his back on a picnic table, getting fucked by Ryan Idol.

"I know," Nick said. "Tim's got good taste."

Scott kept looking back and forth, between the scene on the picnic table and the one outside the television set. Tim had pulled a dildo from under the bed and was using it now to fuck himself as he watched the screen and jerked off with his other hand.

Scott's hand was moving in time to Tim's, he realized suddenly, and for a moment he felt as if Tim were watching *him* jerk off, not the other way around. Scott was the star, the hot body that everyone lusted after, that Tim, with his small dick, was fantasizing about at this very moment.

Nick slapped Scott across the butt, hard. "Wake up. You're taking this all wrong. You need to learn to take it," the ghost said, "up here." He shoved a hand between the cheeks of Scott's ass, pressing upward.

Scott woke up, as ordered, in his own bed again. But not

without one last image of Tim through the television's screen:

Tim was happy as a clam, despite his tiny prick. He screamed and shouted with pleasure, not caring what the neighbors might think as he reveled in the sensations flooding his body. His cum was shooting onto his stomach, pooling in his belly.

Scott's own stomach was slick with semen. Another wet dream, from this second ghost.

He reached down and pushed his wet pajamas down. He ran his fingers through the drying jism, smearing it over his body. He didn't quite have the abandon he'd seen in Tim, thrashing about on the bed, but Scott was enjoying himself. Which is what the ghost had wanted him to learn, he thought.

He lifted his hand to sniff the cum-soaked fingers, and then put them in his mouth. For the first time in years he tasted cum, his own cum, still safe, but reminding him of how much he'd liked the taste of cum, its sweet/salty funk.

Scott left his pajamas on this time and, slightly sticky, rolled over and drifted happily to sleep, one hand clutching his warm, softening cock.

Part Four: Last Offering

Scott stirred as Marvin lifted the covers and climbed into bed beside him. The ghost snuggled up beside Scott, wrapping his arms around his lover. It felt so comfortable, Scott almost believed it was a decade ago, when Marvin was still alive, when he still felt as real as he did right then. Scott didn't want to do anything to break this moment. But he also couldn't help wondering.

"What happened to The Ghost of Christmas Future?" Scott asked, half-asleep.

"I am the ghost of your future," Marvin said.

"And I am the ghost of your future," a second voice said.

Scott looked up, startled by this newcomer. There stood Steven Willis, the first boy he had ever fooled around with, wrestling by the lake at camp one summer and accidentally touching each other's cocks, and deciding they liked it, and touching them again on purpose.

"And I am the ghost of your future," a third voice said. Robert Sutton, his boyfriend from college.

"And I," said the voices, one after another, as every man Scott had ever made love to, had ever dated, had ever sucked off in some tearoom or back alley, had ever fucked or been fucked by, claimed him again.

"But you can't all be dead!" Scott cried. "I know you're not all dead. Eric, I got a Christmas card from you last week, even if I did throw it out. You can't have died between now and then. I didn't even know you were sick!"

"I'm not dead," Eric said, "but I am a ghost of your future. Every time you have sex, you remember all the other men you've had sex with."

"You cannot escape from your past," Marvin said, "nor should you try to. Whenever you make love to another man, I will be with you. And, through you, I will again enjoy the pleasures of life that are now denied me."

"Your abstinence denies not only your own pleasure, but ours as well. We are the ghosts of your future," they cried in unison, every man he had ever loved before, as they climbed into bed with him and ran their fingers, mouths, and cocks across his body.

Scott screamed.

It was too much for him—too much sensation, too much pleasure, too much everything.

But the ghosts did not stop. Voracious and insatiable, they licked and stroked him, holding him down as he struggled beneath them, trying to break free.

His cock was swollen with exertion and excitement, almost despite himself. He did not want to be aroused right then, did not want to be having sex.

But he had no choice. The ghosts took their pleasure from his body, making up for seven long-lost years of enforced vicarious abstinence.

They teased and caressed his body, stroked and petted, pulled and tweaked.

At last, they let him cum—a blindly overwhelming orgasm that knocked him and his overworked senses senseless.

When he awoke, daylight shone through the window. It was Christmas Day. He was naked, atop his bed. White droplets of semen splattered his chest and stomach. "A white Christmas," Scott muttered, with a smile.

He lay on his bed, trying to make sense of his memories of last night, then got up and showered. He dressed and went down to the street.

Recently, the city had been trying to close down all sex establishments—the peep shows and buddy booths, the erotic video arcades and burlesques. Scott had approved of these measures, feeling that such things didn't belong in public, so garish and obvious and present. Sex was something for people to do behind closed doors, if at all.

But his attitudes about sex had changed now. Or rather, changed back, to the way he used to feel.

Scott was glad the city had not succeeded in its attempts to shut down the porno shops, as he headed to the one located two blocks from his apartment. It was open, even on Christmas, for all the dissatisfied and lonely souls needing some quick release on this stressful day.

As Scott entered the XXX-EMPORIUM, he decided to draft

plans for a more upscale pornpalace. Part of the city's problem, Scott thought—aside from the fact that these stores acknowledged that sex, and especially queer sex, existed—was the cheap, no-frills, sleazy way in which they presented and promoted themselves and the entertainments they contained. But if these stores were repackaged, would they stand a better chance of staying alive?

It was worth a try, Scott thought. Even if his plans didn't work, they might get people thinking. It would be his way of contributing to the fight to keep these stores from being forced to close.

Scott bought a dildo to give to Tim—Tiny Tim, he couldn't help recalling, laughing at the irony of it all. The dildo was easily four times the size of Tim's own cock, but that wouldn't bother him at all, Scott was sure. Tim was a piggy little bottom, Scott knew from having watched him masturbate, and his eyes would light up when he unwrapped *this* Christmas gift.

He wondered if he'd use it with Tim sometime. Back when Tim first joined the office, he'd hit on Scott, and Scott had, of course, ignored him at the time.

Now he wondered what it might be like. He considered sex with Tim, even with his tiny prick. Scott was pretty much a bottom, although he was afraid of getting fucked these days, even with a condom. But Tim had fun during sex, that was obvious. Maybe they could have fun together, two bottoms in bed. And, of course, Scott did sometimes like to fuck, and as he stood in the pornshop with his newly awakened sexuality, he felt like he wanted to try everything again.

But thoughts of Tim could wait until later, Scott realized, as he bought the store's largest bottle of lube and a box of condoms for himself. He brought his purchases back to his apartment and put them on the small table just inside the hallway.

Scott sat down at his drafting table and rifled through the papers he had brought home from work the day before. At last, he found what he was looking for and reached for the phone.

"Fred? It's Scott Murphy. Merry Christmas! I was wondering if that offer you made last night was still open...."